THE SPIRIT OF JOSEPHINE

A Novel

The Spirit
of
Josephine

A Family Reunion in Paris

Florence Ladd

Côte-d'Or Press

For
Nancy Holloway,
Dee Dee Bridgewater,
Electra Weston,
and Jamie Bowers,
who are fabulous!

We carry on, in that dingy, musky,
dusty room overhung with fraying
costumes, peeling sequins,
shedding feathers, mules
with broken heels, mending glue, eye-
lash glue, charcoal sticks and matches,
brushes and unguents and bottles of oil.
The dressing room is my schoolhouse.
The beauty is how this strange
trade works. The truth of it is,
we are fabulous.

Elizabeth Alexander, "The Josephine Baker
Museum" in *Body of Life*.

1

Josephine Baker slipped out of heaven and onto my bed again last night. Sometimes she dances. Sometimes she sings. Sometimes she gives advice. Sometimes she just dazzles me with her broad smile. This time, though, she didn't dance and she wasn't smiling. Sitting on the edge of my bed, she looked tired, frumpy, and sad, wearing that down-and-out face she wore in a photograph taken of her on the back steps of her chateau the day she was evicted. What did she want with me this time?

Josephine said, "Violet Fields, I'm here to sing for you." She sang her theme song, "J'ai Deux Amours." Then "Steal Away," she hummed it and then sang the words. Damn! Had she come to Pigalle and rue Frochot to have me steal away with her? Uh-uh, not yet.

I shook myself, struggled out of bed, grabbed my cane, and stood up on these old, swollen legs. But by the time I got to my feet, she'd gone. Motion always sends her away. Just to make sure, I shouted, "Get out of here, Josephine. I ain't ready to steal away yet. So scat!"

She'd already disappeared. A faint aroma, a strange blend of roses and bananas, lingered. On the bedside carpet in my bare feet, I stood wondering why she was calling on me now.

It put me in mind of her first visit. Jean-Louis—he used to be my manager—thinks I have dreams about Josephine. But they don't come to me like dreams. No, they're more like visits with her spirit. She comes to me a dozen or more times a year.

Usually she looks elegant in a skintight silver lamé gown, plumes in her hair, and a white feather boa draped around her.

Long before I came to Paris, Josephine fascinated me. When I was a kid in Louisville, I saw pictures of her in the Negro newspapers and magazines. Like me, she was a poor kid, born to sing and dance. Discovered in New York, she was swept off to Paris where she was a huge success. I was curious about how a colored American woman became a Paris music hall star in the 1920s. When I moved to Paris, nearly everyone I met compared me to her. They told me I could be the next Josephine Baker, although my voice—my throaty alto—was nothing like hers.

The first time she came to me was after a benefit performance I did for a Paris hospital in 1985—twenty years ago. She'd already been dead ten years. Somebody in the fashion industry with a stash of Josephine's costumes had put them up for auction. They needed a model her color and size. I was thin then. Jean-Louis had told the producers that I could imitate her singing. I used to copy her voice, mime her style. He got me the gig. I was wild with excitement about wearing gowns that had been next to her skin.

At the benefit, I sang four of her hit songs, closing with "J'ai Deux Amours," crooning like Josephine. "J'ai deux amours, / Mon pays et Paris. / Par eux toujours, / Mon coeur est ravi."

It was as if she sang through me. I sashayed and flounced the way she used to. In the closing number, draped in a filmy white gown and gliding across the stage, I danced like I've never danced before—or since. I felt possessed.

After the show I went home to get some sleep. Just before dawn, there was a rustling like someone was sitting on my bed. I knew it wasn't Stanley; he was playing with a band in Copenhagen at the time. Besides, it wasn't like Stanley, who got into bed bouncing and rocking the mattress. It was a gentler motion. And it wasn't the cat either; it was a lighter movement even than old Leona's. I woke up, my eyes wide open. I saw an oval glow of pale blue light, and sitting in the middle of it was Josephine. She said, "You sang my songs beautifully. *Merci*, Violet." Then she sang in her light, airy style "Show Business" and "J'ai Deux Amours." I lay there trembling. Before fading into the oval light, she said, "I'll pass your way again." The odor of a fruity perfume floated by me.

Mind you, I was over fifty years old, and in all those years, nothing like that had ever happened to me. I didn't traffic with spirits. My mother's ghost never visited me. Little Stanley Junior, the baby we lost, never haunted me either. When a heart attack took Stanley two years ago, I hoped he'd pay me a visit, but there's been no sign of him. Only Josephine comes to me.

She doesn't visit at random times. There's always some occasion like her birthday, June 3, or mine the next day; both Gemini. She comes in April, around the anniversary of her death. The night after my last gig—a few years ago—she appeared at the foot of my bed.

I can't imagine why she visited last night. Everything seems routine right now, or as routine as things are in Paris in August when it's so damn hot. Nobody's in the city, nobody except tourists. The routine of trying to stay alive is what's keeping me here: visiting my doctor, taking my insulin, checking my blood pressure. And my daily chores: feeding Leo (the calico stray I took in after Leona died), washing my underwear, watching TV quiz shows, playing solitaire, going downstairs for the mail and across the street to the café. When I have time, I think about putting my photos and souvenirs in some kind of order and trying to track down my nieces in the States.

Jean-Louis is coming back tonight or tomorrow. I wish I'd gone with him to Avignon. I'd like to see Avignon, Antibes, and Cannes again, and get to Monaco. Someday I'll go to Monaco, see where they buried Josephine—visit the grave where that spirit of hers is not resting in peace.

When Jean-Louis comes, he'll have a reason for Josephine's appearance last night. He'll find something hopeful in her singing "Steal Away." I don't like the idea of stealing away to Jesus, not just yet. Not ready to audition for that show. Maybe I should go to church, although it's easier to put a camel through the eye of a needle than to find a church in Paris that speaks to my Baptist soul.

The last time I went into a church to pray—not counting weddings, funerals, and gospel concerts— was in April, 1975, right after Josephine's funeral at the magnificent church, La Madeleine, a week after her final show at the Bobino. Thousands of mourners were jammed in the street below the church. In the crowd, I got only a glimpse of her casket draped in France's flag to honor her service in World War II.

When her coffin was carried away and the crowd thinned, I climbed the steep steps, went inside the church, sat in a pew, and prayed for Josephine's talent to touch me. A huge statue of the Madonna and child was on my left and, opposite on my right, a statue of Jesus. Above the altar was a dumpling-

4

plump statue of the Virgin Mary surrounded by angels. In her marble features I saw Josephine's face!

I left La Madeleine and came back here to our apartment where I went through my collection of clippings, photographs, and postcards of Josephine. I selected a few, put them on the corner table in the bedroom, and made myself an altar dedicated to my own personal Saint Josephine. The altar is bigger now, as I've added more pictures of her. When I need inspiration, I visit the pictures: Josephine in a long silk evening gown edged with lace; posing nude with her hands over her breasts, a scarf and a rope of pearls draped in front; naked except for a belt of bananas; seated among huge feathers with only a necklace over her bare breasts; in a skimpy bathing suit of pearls; lounging in a bubble bath; and my favorite, Josephine in top hat, white tie, and cutaway coat. I light little candles in front of her pictures.

Stanley didn't like having the altar in our bedroom, but he never asked me to take it down. He said I "overly admired" her, made too much of what she'd accomplished. I used to tell him, "Hey, Stanley, I wouldn't be singing in clubs and cabarets in Paris if Josephine hadn't lit the way."

Daylight's coming in an hour or so. The racket of the ninth arrondissement—neighbors throwing open shutters and rolling up steel grills of shops—will wake me, that is, if I can get to sleep before facing what Josephine has in store for me today.

2

"*Attendez. J'arrive*! Must be somebody who doesn't know I don't like to see folks before noon. Knocking so loud, it's somebody who thinks I'm hard of hearing." In the semidarkness, I reach for my cane. Under the heap of clothes on the chest at the foot of my bed, I find my red silk kimono. "I'm not deaf. I'm coming."

It takes me a while to hobble from the bedroom, through the living room, and down the hall to the foyer. I turn on the light, glance at the mirror, and see it's hair-tinting time again. My hennaed Afro is growing out; the roots are white. The Garfield gap between my front teeth is widening; puffiness under my eyes and pudgy cheeks. At the neckline of my kimono, the frayed lace of this old-time nightgown is showing. No way to greet a stranger.

"*J'arrive!*" I shout, turning the three locks. I open the door slightly and peep through the crack before unhooking the chain. "Jean-Louis, am I glad you're back!" I open the door, step aside to make way for the entrance of Boris, his Russian wolfhound, and then reach up to hug Jean-Louis. Even in the dim light of the hall, I can see he's not his usual crisp self. His clothes look like he's slept in them; the tan linen jacket and blue jeans are wrinkled. Under the jacket, his trademark black T-shirt is soup stained. He hasn't brushed the thin, gray strands over his baldness. There's no liner around his watery, brown eyes. He looks even more haggard than he did before he went on vacation. Our cheeks brush in an exchange of kisses. I notice he hasn't shaved for a day or two.

"You look like you had a very bad trip. What's happened?"

6

"I drove all night. When I reached Paris, I went to my place to leave my luggage, and regard my mail. *Alors*, immediately I came here to see you. All the time, I was worrying about you. Are you going well?" Jean-Louis's blend of French and English amuses me. His Provençal accent makes it hard to understand him, no matter which language he speaks. Still, I can tolerate his English better than he tolerates my French. He says my speaking French with a Kentucky accent is *insupportable* – unbearable.

"I'm all right. Nothing much has changed. You were gone only a week."

"I returned to see what you need. Groceries, something from the pharmacy? What do you need?"

"I need to tell you about Josephine's visit last night."

"*Alors*. What did she do this time?" He's always eager to hear about Josephine.

"Come on in and I'll tell you. I'll make coffee."

"No, I will make the coffee." He stops to light a cigarette and give me time to walk along the hall, through a storage area that used to be the dining room, and into the kitchen. The dining table is covered with stacks of mail, magazines, scrapbooks, and photo albums; boxes are stored under the table. Newspapers and magazines are piled on all six dining room chairs. So we have to sit in the kitchen.

The kitchen is narrow and tight as the galley of a sailboat, with just enough room for a café table and two chairs near the kitchen door. That's where we usually begin—in the kitchen where we have conversations about our *grands projets*. A TV program may take us into the bedroom where the television set is, but Jean-Louis and I usually gravitate toward the kitchen. Boris follows us and lies down at my feet from where he can see Jean-

7

Louis and look up occasionally at Leo, perched atop the refrigerator.

Except for some cups, a soup bowl, and spoons in the sink, the kitchen is in good order. Jean-Louis knows my place almost as well as I do. He dips into the coffee canister and says, "There's only enough for one cup. I'll have *vin blanc* instead." He fills the coffee maker, turns it on, and opens the frigo where he finds an opened bottle of Chablis. He pours a glass, places an ashtray and the glass on the table, and sits in the other chair facing me. Puffing a Gauloise, he flashes an impatient glance at the coffeemaker as it hisses and gurgles. He knows I'm not going to say a word about Josephine until my morning coffee is under my nose. He stares at me, his horn-rimmed lenses magnifying his gaze. While we wait for the coffee to brew, Jean-Louis does his routine checkup.

"Have you been eating regularly?"

"Oui, monsieur."

"Did you take the insulin everyday?"

"Oui, monsieur."

"And record your blood sugar test results?"

"Oui, monsieur."

"Checked for hypertension?"

"Oui, monsieur."

"Did you promenade? Do your exercises?"

"Oui, monsieur," I say, although he knows that I've only walked up and down the two flights of stairs in my building and across the street to the café for my daily Coke Light. I call it my *apéritif.*

Watching the coffee trickle into the carafe, Jean-Louis lights another cigarette off the one he's finishing. I'm still mulling over Josephine's visit. After a few minutes, he gets up, fills a cup, brings it to me, sits down, and says, *"Alors?"*

I close my eyes, breathe in the perfume of coffee before sipping it, and say, "Josephine came, sat on the bed, and sang to me the spiritual 'Steal Away.'" In an imitation of her soprano, I sing, "Steal away / Steal away / Steal away to Jesus / Steal away / Steal away home / I ain't got long to stay here." I pause and stare at him. "She really scared me this time. She looked tired—like she's tired of coming to see me. What do you think she's telling me?"

He repeats the lyrics, "Steal away / steal away home" then says matter-of-factly, "Well, it is obvious. She is telling you that you should leave Paris and return to America."

"Paris is my home. When I moved here in '52, I was already stealing away, baby, getting out from under old Jim Crow, following Josephine's footsteps. She didn't go back to St. Louis. She stayed here, died here. So Josephine wouldn't be telling me to go back to Louisville." I pause for a sip of coffee. "Maybe you think I ought to return to the States. But there's nobody there for me. Here at least I've got you and my three backup girls."

"You cannot depend on those chorus girls. They are fans. Fans are fickle. Claire, I believe, is leaving next week to be a dancer on a cruise ship."

"So my two backups." As I say it, I know I might be down to one if Odile joins her boyfriend in Antibes. But Monique, who's from an old Paris family, will probably stay here. "Monique's got her papa's car all month. She's been taking me here and there. She said she'll come around more often, if I'm too much trouble for you."

"Violetta, you are no trouble at all." He never calls me Violet. He says I should have kept my original name. Being called Violetta, he said, would have bettered my career. More than once, he's told me it would remind listeners of Violetta in La Traviata.

Jean-Louis says, "You know that I do not want you to go to America. I do not go to live with my sisters in Provence. I stay here to be with you. To care for you. That is what old friends must do for each other, Violetta. *Alors*, perhaps Josephine is telling you something else."

"I know what 'Steal Away' means. She's telling me to get ready to die. Church choirs sing that number at funerals. And she sang it mournful-like."

"We must find other meanings. Tell me, what was she wearing this time?"

"You know the photograph of her when she was evicted from the chateau? Barefooted, eyes downcast, sitting outside on the back steps?"

"But of course, wearing a shower cap, baggy sweater, blanket for a skirt, satchel at her side. Who can forget that image?" he sighs.

"Well, that's how she came this time. Looking her down-on-her-luck worst—like I'm feeling." I glance up at the ceiling puckered by leaks and the walls where paint is peeling. My kitchen looks the way I feel.

"Sitting on the steps! That's the clue. Someone's coming to your steps."

"A doctor? An undertaker?"

"Do not become morbid, Violetta. I believe she is telling you to expect a visitor on your steps."

I roll my eyes and shake my head. "Maybe she's saying I should move—steal away to another apartment. It's rumored this building may be renovated. You think I could be evicted?"

"Josephine was evicted, but it was not the end for her. She had her grand finale."

"And then she died."

"We all die eventually, Violetta."

"Well, I've got a few things to do before eventually comes."

"And I have a few things to do today. What do you need from the market?" Tilting his head back to drain his glass, he exposes his wattled neck. His right hand trembles as he places the glass on the table. I'm wondering if I should be relying on Jean-Louis for errands. He's three years older than I am, has the shakes, and is awfully forgetful.

"I made a list yesterday, but I don't remember where I put it," I tell him.

"*Alors*, I know it by heart: bananas, butter, marmalade, milk, bread, cheese, toilet paper. And you need coffee."

"Let me give you some euros."

"I will add it on your account."

"What account? You're not keeping any records."

"*Mais oui.* My neighbor, Gérard, the pretty boy I told you about, has computerized my financial records. He is a computer genius. Did you see his photo?" He pulls his wallet from a pocket in his jacket.

"I've seen that dog-eared picture I don't know how many times."

"Gérard can locate people anywhere in the world on the Internet. I told him you want to find your nieces—Faith and Hope—religious names. But I forget their family name. Tell me again and he will find them."

"Grayson. There's a pad of paper on the counter. Write down their names." He reaches for the pad and takes a pen from the pocket of his jacket. Slowly, like dictating to a secretary, I tell him, "The older one is Faith Grayson. Aunt Olivia, in her last letter before she died, wrote that Faith had gone to some college in Ohio and stayed there. The younger one, Hope Grayson, is probably still in Louisville. The last time I saw them was fifteen years ago, at their father's funeral."

"The funeral where your sister made the jealousy scene?"

"Yes, indeed, Marie was jealous and angry. Accused me of upstaging her at her husband's burial. She always felt I stole the show. At the graveside, somebody called out, 'Miss Violet, sing "Abide with Me." I smiled, shook my head. Marie, standing opposite me on the other side of the casket, lifted her veil from her face and said, 'I don't want your kind of singing here.'"

Like Mama, Marie frowned on show business. Mama used to say, "Lifting your legs isn't uplifting the race."

"What more did Marie say?" Jean-Louis asks, although he's heard the story dozens of times.

"She said, 'You always have to be the main event. I'm sorry you came. I don't want you visiting again.' She started her hysterical crying. The undertaker's aide put her arm around Marie to calm her. Then without being prompted at all, the young one, Hope, lifted her head and with a clear voice and dry eyes, that little girl sang. At her daddy's funeral, she sang 'Amazing Grace,' a cappella with perfect pitch, trills, and vibrato on just the right notes. I choke up just thinking about how her voice silenced everybody, including Marie.

"Hope was only nine years old at the time. I sure would like to know what she's done with that voice. You think your friend, Gérard, can find her?"

"Of course he can find her. When he locates her address and telephone number, what will you do?"

Jean-Louis lifts his shoulders in what I call the French shrug, as if to say, "So what?"

"I'll phone her. If she wants to know about me, I'll pack up some photographs of myself, programs, clippings, my albums and CDs, and ship them over to her. It's all I have to pass on. I want my nieces to know about me. I want their names listed in my obituary. It makes me sad to read that somebody died with no survivors."

"But you have a sister and your brother. He may be alive somewhere."

"Marie disrespected me in public—at that funeral. She's no sister to me."

"Perhaps your brother is still alive in Korea. You used to speak of him warmly."

"If Hampton's alive, he doesn't know if I'm living or dead. I haven't heard from him in years. If I die tomorrow, I've got nobody as next of kin, no one to claim me."

"Do not go morbid, Violetta." Jean-Louis gets up. Boris unfolds his legs, stands, and shakes himself. "I must do the shopping. I will bring for lunch the artichoke terrine my sister made. At lunch I will tell you my idea for a Christmas show with you singing a program of carols and Negro spirituals."

"The doctor's telling me he may have to cut off my left leg. And you're thinking of putting me onstage in a Christmas program? I can see the marquee: GO TELL IT ON THE MOUNTAIN WITH PEG-LEG VIOLET FIELDS!"

"Keep on the diet, keep taking the medicine, and keep your leg. When I come back, we will talk about the show. I will stop at the market. What should I buy for your dinner?"

"I'm having dinner out—at a Senegalese restaurant tonight with Odile and Monique. Want to join us?"

"Not tonight. I am going with some old British queens to pub crawl, as they say."

I lean on the table to lift myself up. Jean-Louis, his hands trembling, tries to steady the table. Boris leads the way to the door. As they start down the stairs, I call out, "Will you bring up the mail when you come back?"

"No, walk down and get it yourself. You need the exercise."

I always ask him to bring up the mail; and Jean-Louis always refuses. Just getting dressed in the morning—and it takes nearly all morning—is enough exercise. Damn!

3

Every morning before getting dressed, I spend some time with Stanley—that is, with photos of Stanley and his bands. Stanley framed and hung all of them. It's a parade of his life, from the time he played the trumpet in a Baltimore high school marching band to his last gig in a Paris music hall. At first he placed pictures on only one wall. After each show, he'd hang up another photograph. Labeled each one with the name of the group, place, and date. By the time he died, his music scenes filled all the space on all four walls in our living room. Every time we had company, Stanley toured his career for our guests. He loved to point out pictures of himself with our royalty: Basie and Ellington. He told wonderful stories about playing in Havana for the Castros, having his trumpet stolen in Lagos, and audiences in Tokyo. Jean-Louis calls the room Stanley's pantheon. I come in here, walk around, and look for Stanley in each picture. He's taller than most in the groups. "Tall, tan, and taciturn Stan" was how Basie always introduced him.

This daily tour is my revival hour. It makes me feel Stanley's still alive, just out of town playing a gig somewhere. First, I stop in front of this picture of Stanley with one arm around me, his trumpet on the other arm. Stanley wrote in the margin, "Violetta Garfield (aka Violet Fields) with Stanley, US Embassy, Paris, July 4, 1952."

I'd come to Paris with the show New Faces 1952. It opened in March and closed in April. When the show ended, the rest of cast went back to New York. I'd come over with most of my belongings—my clothes, junk jewelry, favorite records. I'd saved enough francs to cover a few months for a room in a cheap Left Bank hotel near the Sorbonne on rue Cujas and meals of bread, Camembert, and *vin ordinaire*. I was poor and Paris felt poor, too. Still recovering from World War II and the Nazi occupation, she was like a grand lady who had hidden her finery and was gradually finding her evening slippers, feather boas, her genuine pearls. Shop fronts were being painted; placards in front of restaurants advertised their fare: *vol-au-vent, salade,* and *baba au rhum* for very few francs—but more than I could afford. Admiring delicacies displayed in *charcuterie* and *patisserie* windows and deeply inhaling whenever I passed a *boulangerie* had to satisfy my appetite.

I had a favorite table at Café St. Michel where I lingered over an afternoon cup of coffee or glass of *vin rouge*. Eavesdropping on conversations I couldn't understand, still I was fascinated by the intensity of scholarly types and their flurry of words, words I assumed were about ideas, the arts, and important books. Flirtatious French men—some young and others timeworn and tattered—seated themselves at the table next to mine and tried to make conversation. My repeating a useful phrase, "*Non, merci,*" usually discouraged them. Evenings found me making the rounds of clubs and cabarets looking for work.

Stanley and I met that June at a cabaret where I was auditioning. He liked my voice, said it was warm and mellow. His combo was booked at the American Embassy for the Fourth, and they needed *une chanteuse*—a girl to sing "Summertime." I jumped at the chance. I sang it in a slow, melancholy style. The crowd loved it, but Stanley really grooved on it, and that's what mattered.

Afterward we feasted on the Embassy's hot dogs and Cokes. When the party was over, Stanley said he wanted to show me his Paris. At dusk along the Champs-Elysées, we joined the procession of natives and tourists strolling toward Place de la Concorde. Stanley took my hand and guided me across streets to a wall near the Orangerie. Just as we paused to watch the traffic rumble around the obelisk, lights flooded the monument; its dancing fountains shimmered. "It's gorgeous!" I said. Stanley said, "It's places like this that make Paris gorgeous. Let's walk over to the Petit Palais and the Grand Palais." The Petit Palais looked pretty grand to me; and Grand Palais was colossal. Stanley talked about art exhibitions he had seen at one of the palaces. It was after hours so they were closed. He said he'd take me there sometime to see an art show. A couple seated on the steps of the Grand Palais was locked in an embrace and an endless kiss. "Only in Paris," I said, but Stanley didn't reply with the kiss I wanted.

We crossed a bridge to the Left Bank and strolled along the *quai*, stopping from time to time to notice boats ripple along the Seine, their lights shimmering on the water; stopping to scan the books, posters, and postcards of a *bouquiniste*; stopping to admire the towers of Notre Dame from a distance. Along the narrow streets off Place St. Michel, Stanley and I slowed our pace to take in the aroma of roasted lamb wafting from Greek and Turkish restaurants. Stanley said, "You can get a fine, four-course meal in one of those places for the equivalent of a dollar."

In the Latin Quarter, at almost midnight cafés were bustling with people. Street singers were on every other corner. When we reached my hotel, a one-star joint on rue Cujas, I said maybe I should turn in. Stanley lifted my chin, kissed me, and said he was enjoying my company.

"Let's get a drink at Café Monaco," he said. "It's a hangout for Negro refugees from American segregation."

"Are you a refugee?"

"An accidental refugee. Not like some brothers from the deep South—more southern than Baltimore. From Alabama, Mississippi, Georgia, where they'd have to bow and scrape for the Man, hunker down, settle for being downtrodden and dirt poor again. After the war they stayed on here. Me, I went back to the States."

Stanley was in the U.S. Navy during the war, on a destroyer in the North Atlantic. On shore leave, he'd hang out and jam in clubs in Bergen, Copenhagen, and Stockholm. He said, "I'd be there with my horn. Scandinavian band leaders took notice of a black musician, called me up to jam with them."

"Did you think of staying there after the war?" I wondered.

"Nope. I went back to Baltimore. I was thinking of going to college to study music on the G.I. Bill. Applied to Howard, was admitted, but I didn't get there."

"What happened?"

"I got a summons, so to speak. Got recalled to Stockholm," he groaned.

"A band wanted you?"

"No, a woman. Thought she was pregnant at the time. I came over, married her. That's what I mean about being an accidental refugee. Turns out she wasn't pregnant. Wasn't until we were breaking up that she had a baby. A girl, Margareta. She's three and a half now. When I get a chance, I go to Stockholm and see her." We stopped under a streetlight. Stanley took a snapshot from his wallet showing me a fair-skinned, angelic looking baby with kinky, blond hair.

"She's cute. Are you still married?"

"Trying to work out a divorce."

Damn! It didn't matter though. I'd already fallen for him. I liked the way he blew complex solos that made you think about the music, not just feel it. He was smart about the new jazz. He was refined, had gentlemanly manners and a dignified air. Like Basie said, he was tall, tan, and taciturn. He was talented, too. And he had a mustache that I wanted to tickle my lips.

"You've got a fine voice, foxy looks, gorgeous body, and you're young—how old?" He slipped an arm around my waist.

"Twenty."

"Do you really think you can hack it here?"

"Why not? Paris has been good to Negro entertainers in the past." I was thinking of Josephine Baker and musicians in the twenties and thirties who'd made it in Paris. "I'll find work as a singer or dancer or both. I audition any time I have the chance."

"So you think you'll stay?"

In my first week here, promenading along the boulevards, going in and out of shops, lingering over a drink at a bar or café, I knew I wanted to stay. I felt free, like I'd been untied from something I didn't know was holding me down.

"Here I feel liberated," I said.

"Liberated? Are you another one of those Negro Americans who thinks the French are color-blind?" Stanley asked.

"No, they see my color, they see my hair, but it doesn't seem to matter. I get the same respect they show everybody else. Anyhow, I want to stay liberated, keep some distance from America's racial hang-ups and my own hang-ups about unfinished family business. I've got family in Kentucky—in Louisville."

"The unfinished business—what's that about?"

"Bickering with my mom about singing and dancing. When my daddy had an accident that killed him, I wasn't there. I feel guilty about leaving my brother, Hampton, there to deal with a wicked situation. And I've got a little sister there."

"You think you might go back to Louisville to finish that business?"

"Not likely. What about you? Will you move back to the States someday?"

"Back to Baltimore? Never. If I went, I'd probably be recalled for service in Korea. Or I'd be summoned by McCarthy's Un-American Activities Committee. A Negro with a Swedish wife and kid is probably an un-American activity," he chuckled.

We reached rue Monsieur-le-Prince and the Café Monaco just as it was closing. Some cats with instrument cases were leaving. They hailed Stanley and asked to be introduced to his "new chick." With his arm around me, holding me close, Stanley told them I was his discovery. He didn't tell them my name. One of them said, "Man, you didn't discover her. I saw her in New Faces 1952 a few weeks ago. She came from New York with the show. Too bad it had a short run here. You did a great scene, darling."

Stanley said, "You'll be seeing her again. She's going to sing with my combo." He steered me away from the group. We walked aimlessly—or so I thought—for a while. On rue Saint-Benoit, we stopped in front of a small hotel. He started singing, "Darling, Je Vous Aime Beaucoup," in the style of Nat King Cole. I was enchanted. Ending his serenade, he said, "This is where I'm staying. "Come on in, baby. I've got some tapes I want you to hear— and a good bottle of bourbon."

That night I fell in love with Stanley, and I fell in love with Paris.

***

For a few years, we had frequent gigs together at Caveau de la Huchette, a jazz club near Place St. Michel. On the street level, there was a quiet, dimly lit bar with a few tables. Downstairs in what once had been a wine cellar was a postage-stamp-size bandstand and a dance floor that wasn't much bigger. A middle-aged bourgeois crowd that loved to jitterbug and swing dance filled the place. All the seats at the tiny, marble-topped café tables around the dance floor were taken before the show started.

Latecomers stood crammed in corners and on the stairs. Clouds of cigarette smoke shaded rose-colored lights.

Stanley on trumpet with his combo—a saxophone, guitar, double bass, and percussion— warmed up the crowd. After the waitress served drinks and Stanley sensed the crowd was laid-back, he introduced me: "Violet Fields—America's gift to Paris and God's gift to me." I'd swish onstage in my black sequined gown. Stanley kissed my hand and ushered me to the mike. He altered the tempo of the music to match my phrasing, the pitch to suit my voice. My repertoire included some of Josephine's songs and other Paris favorites. At the end of the program, I crooned "The Man I Love," my eyes fixed on Stanley. After every show, he'd say, "Violet, you've got great vocal chords and vocal hips." And I'd tell him, "You've got the sweetest lips that ever kissed a horn." I loved watching him play, tilting his trumpet up and blowing notes that fell over a crowd like confetti.

We romanced each other onstage more faithfully than we did in real life. Living together was rocky at first. Lots of women had eyes for Stanley—and his resistance was low. I got upset about his trips to Stockholm. We'd break up when I was hurt, jealous, and angry. I'd move out of the hotel where we were living, find a room of my own. I dated other guys when we were apart, but I didn't get any kicks from sleeping around. If Stanley was concerned about my two-timing him, he never mentioned it—except when I asked if he'd been cheating on me. He'd say, "You feeling guilty, ashamed about cheating on me?" Time and time again, music helped us make up. We'd have a gig together and groove onstage. I'd try to forget whatever had happened, and we'd end the night making love.

After a while, he settled down, and we were a steady couple. Eventually, seven years after we met, Stanley got divorced, and we slow danced into marriage. We had a civil ceremony at city hall. Afterwards, we celebrated at the Blue Note with two sax players and their girlfriends, our witnesses. We're all in that gold frame on the wall over there. By that time, he was in a band that played in the best Paris clubs and in festivals all over France. We quit staying in shoddy Left Bank hotels and moved here to this apartment in the ninth arrondissement, the center of *joie de vivre* in Paris. We owned a Citroen and dressed *à la mode*. The good times were rolling.

I wrote to Mama with our wedding news, sent her one of the photos taken that day. She never responded—not a card, not a word from her. It was downright painful to know she didn't care enough for me to recognize my marriage. Still pains me when I think of it.

What saddens me most are three pictures in that corner. In the one up top, I'm standing sideways, obviously very pregnant. Below it, the picture of Stanley and me taken a few weeks later. We're smiling proudly, with me holding our baby, little Stanley. We were, at last, a family. He was thrilled about having a son, dreamed of a grand future in jazz for the boy. I was happy to be breast-feeding and cuddling. I enjoyed being needed. Little Stanley failed to gain weight and developed a chronic fever. I realized then that his life mattered more to me than my own. They couldn't save him. In the photo framed in a ceramic wreath is our last picture of little Stanley.

We never recovered from the loss. Soon afterwards, Stanley learned that he had a weak heart. I knew it had been weakened by the death of our baby. Still we weren't prepared for Stanley's heart attack. When he was taken to the hospital, I tried to reach Margareta, his daughter. I left messages at all the Stockholm numbers in his little black book. Nobody called back.

At the graveside service at Montmartre Cemetery, Archibald Davis, minister-turned-musician, preached what he called his requiem sermon about Stanley as a missionary in music. Jimmy Brooks played a medley of spirituals on his clarinet. Whatever else happened was blurred by my tears. I wish somebody had taken pictures that day.

This living room needs to be painted. But I'd have to take all Stanley's pictures down, keep the right labels with them. And then what? Hang them up again? Somebody said I ought to find a library or jazz museum that might want them. But I don't want to part with them. They bring back memories. I miss the music of Stanley's horn. Recordings just don't deliver the true sound, the real thing. Seeing these pictures reminds me of how full this life once was. Now it's a gloomy, old museum.

Fixing up and painting the bedroom would be a good project. The windows are dirty, the quilt tattered, the draperies faded—you'd never know they were once a lovely shade of blue. Both armoires are bulging with costumes and everyday clothes. Heaps of skirts and dresses are on the chairs. I don't wear them now; I need pants to hide my varicose veins.

This bedroom looks like a stage set for a deathbed scene. No wonder Josephine is telling me to steal away to Jesus. If I'm going to live, this place ought to look like somebody with a future is living here. If I'm going to die, I ought to leave it just like it is—watch it grow more shabby, the kind of place where one might find a dead body.

4

"Dining out with you girls is always a trip, but this takes the cake. How in the world did you girls find this funky place?" I survey the interior of the Senegalese restaurant. It's a gloomy, candlelit cavern. On a hot August night, it's not the kind of place I'd choose for dinner.

"Odile found it. This is my first time here," says Monique who, for practice, talks to me in her BBC English. She wants no responsibility for the venue, in an immigrant quarter of the eighteenth arrondissement. Odile, still at the entrance, is speaking with the waiter.

I met Odile and Monique in a cabaret show where I sang a few numbers. I couldn't tell them apart. Lean, dark-haired dancers—they look so much alike that they're often taken for sisters.

I count ten square tables covered with oilcloth, each with a different pattern; four chairs at each table, crowding the room. We're the only customers. Monique and I take a corner table. A barefoot boy in shorts and a T-shirt appears, squats near our table, and plays a tuneless tune on a thumb piano. From the kitchen, the sound of oil sizzling in a frying pan competes with his tinkling the tin tines.

Odile finally joins us. "Youssouf recommends the red snapper tonight," she says.

"How'd you hear about this place?" I ask, wondering why Odile has brought us here. We drove by several attractive restaurants with sidewalk tables before we came to this place.

"A dancer I met at an audition last week—a black American—recommended it. She wants to meet you, Violet. She is joining us for dinner."

"Why does she want to meet me?"

"I told her about you. She wants to learn about show business here. She is curious about how you made it in Paris," Odile says.

I take a deep breath. Just thinking about the route from Louisville to Paris is exhausting.

"*Alors*, she looks like you when you were her age, the way you looked in the pictures taken at your early shows. She has the same eyes, same nose. Besides, she said you may be related to her." Odile says this as if to surprise me, and it does.

"Really? What's her name?"

"Greta," Odile says.

"Greta? That's a German name. That's no name for a black American girl. No Gretas in my family. What's her last name?"

"I did not ask her."

"Where is she from?" Monique wants to know.

"Atlanta in Georgia," Odile says, pronouncing the place names slowly.

"I don't have any kinfolk in Atlanta." I light a cigarette and look across the table at Odile. "And I don't fancy telling my story to some stranger—even if she is black."

The boy who'd been playing the thumb piano brings a tray with glasses of beer. With a clink of glasses, we say, "*Santé.*"

Monique says, "Odile may know, but I don't know how you got into show business."

I take a long swallow of beer and think of Mabel Henderson. "I'll tell you the short version. An older Louisville girl became the hottest dancer in Saratoga, New York. She was going to New York City to try out for shows. She told me to move to New York with her.

"I went to New York in '48, long before you girls were born. I lived with Mabel. Vets who'd been overseas had come home to Harlem. They had big ideas and a few bucks. New clubs were opening. At first, I worked as a cigarette girl in a club. On weekends Mabel and I went to parties with musicians, artists, and writers. We drank cheap whisky, smoked reefer, told lies about our pasts, and fantasized about the future.

"At home Mabel and I practiced the routines of the Radio City Music Hall Rockettes, a big chorus line. One day I saw the Rockettes' call in *Variety* for dancers. Mabel had told me they only hired white girls. But I went downtown anyway, signed in, and got in line. When my turn came, the audition director said, 'Sorry, we don't have Negro girls in the show. Don't bother to do your routine. It's a waste of your time and mine.' I was really hurt, I mean crushed. I didn't want to go on being a cigarette girl. Luckily, I got a chance to try out for a show at the Apollo Theater in Harlem. They liked my style, hired me for their chorus line. It was 1950. I'd just turned eighteen. Two years later, I'm in Paris with a show— New Faces 1952. That was fifty-five years ago. Blows my mind, remembering the way things happened for me." Between sips of beer, I ask, "How old is this Greta?"

"In her twenties," Odile says with a glance at her watch.

"Maybe she's changed her mind," I say.

"Try phoning her again, Odile," Monique urges.

Just as Odile takes her cell phone from her handbag and dials, Youssouf brings our food: steaming plates of fish smothered in an onion, tomato, pepper, and peanut sauce and a huge bowl of rice. "*Une assiette traditionnelle,*" he tells us in a husky Senegalese accent. While Odile has a brief exchange on the phone, Monique and I start eating.

27

The food is tasty. Another mouthful, and I murmur, "This is delicious." The ambiance no longer matters.

Odile says, "Greta cannot join us. She has a modeling job tonight. She wants to meet you tomorrow afternoon. I will bring her to your apartment."

"Not to my apartment. No way. I'll meet her at the café across the street."

I don't want somebody I'm meeting for the first time to see my place in a jumble. These young people want to know all about you, get inside your skin. They even want to get inside your apartment.

5

After dinner Monique drives Odile and me to a Métro station. In late evening it's usually cooler, but tonight Paris is still sizzling. The Métro is full of tourists—Americans, Germans, Italians, and Japanese. We have to stand, and my feet are killing me. I stare at a young Japanese fellow, wondering what's happened to his respect for elders. He knows why I'm looking at him, gets up, and gives me his seat.

At Pigalle, Odile is patient as I climb the Métro stairs one step at a time, resting on my cane halfway up. It's almost midnight. Hordes of people are roaming the streets. That's what I like about living near Pigalle. The scene is buzzing, jumping day and night, but especially at night. When I was working, I could come home in the wee hours of the morning feeling safe. Lots of people were on the prowl, in and out of the sex shows, working the action. I used to know all the regulars, but I don't know many now. A new set of hookers, drag queens, hustlers, pimps, and johns occupies the streets. Neon signs and photographs of new naked girls advertise the "exotic" shows. Most of them aren't exotic or artistic, just raunchy. Tourists stroll up and down, gaping and glaring—looking for thrills. For me, it's ordinary life. It's my neighborhood.

It's funky—my *quartier*. It's not a clean as some streets in the ninth arrondissement. A lot of folks have dogs, so I have to watch my step on the sidewalk. Every day a platoon of workers in green vests flushes the gutters; before they finish, a new layer of rubbish accumulates. Tourists don't care about the environment. They come here for sexual thrills.

My heart goes out to some of the girls—the young ones especially, and all the black hookers. Paris has been their destination, their dream. Girls come here from everywhere—Haiti, Mali, Thailand, Vietnam, Russia, Poland, Turkey, Egypt—looking for a better life, a taste of freedom. They don't find real work, get down on their luck, and take to the streets.

We cross to the corner where Olga from Siberia hangs out. Speaking some French and a little English, she came on the scene last winter. Seeing us, she waves her red scarf, a big, silk square. She uses it like a matador's cape to stop cars. Olga usually wears a red sheath dress and matching shoes with stiletto heels, but tonight she's in black.

"*Bonsoir*, Madame Violet," she says with a grin showing that a front tooth is now missing. She's rouged a bruise on her left cheek.

"*Bonsoir*, Olga. Why the black dress? Did a rich client die?" She and I double over with laughter. Odile doesn't find it funny. With raised eyebrows and pursed lips, Odile reminds me that she doesn't like it when I chat with the prostitutes.

"My friend, Anna, give me dress. She go back to Russia. She could not deal in business here. You like dress?"

"It looks good on you. *Bonsoir*." I nod and *bonsoir* other girls as we walk toward my building where Sylvia, the gypsy fortuneteller, has the apartment on the street level. A red and green neon sign, *Médium et Tarot*, flashes in her window. At the café across the street, a waiter is placing chairs on tables.

"I'd ask you to join me for a drink over there, but they're closing."

"Let me walk upstairs with you," Odile says.

30

"No, thanks. I'll be fine. Bring your friend, Greta, tomorrow at four. Meet me over there at the café. Call to remind me. The memory isn't what it used to be." I tap my right temple. Odile waits while I enter the code numbers that unlock the door. She kisses my cheeks and heads up the street for the Métro.

Standing in the vestibule, I look at the steps. The climb is slower, harder every time. I pause on the seventh step. It's not a climb; it's an ascent. Finally at my door, I hear Leo whining inside. Did I forget to leave food for him?

In the kitchen I see that Leo has eaten most of the fishy morsels I put in his dish. I get out of my clothes and slip on a nightgown and turn on the TV, to be lulled to sleep by its hum and the glow from the screen. I'm exhausted, but what to tell this Greta keeps me awake.

6

The following day, Jean-Louis arrives, mimicking my hoarse, early morning voice. In the recorded message I said, "Jean-Louis, please bring me a shampoo for color-treated hair, henna tint, and a midnight blue nail polish. And come early—around noon." His imitation makes me chuckle. He hands me a bag from my favorite store, Monoprix. As he follows me into the kitchen, Boris brushes by us, chasing Leo to his perch.

"I am curious about your shopping list," he says. "Are you having a rendezvous with someone?"

"I'm meeting a girl from the States, a dancer. She wants advice about getting into the entertainment scene here. It's given me a case of nerves." I pour him a glass of Chablis, and a Coke Light for myself. We raise glasses and together say, "*Santé*." For us it's more a prayer than a toast.

"Why are you nervous about meeting this girl?"

"What can I tell her about the music hall and club scene? It's not what it was years ago. I don't know any of the players now."

"If she needs a manager, perhaps I can assist her." He lifts his shoulders in his white linen jacket and stretches his neck like a bantam cock. He sees my sympathetic glance. Lighting a cigarette he says, "I have a talent for management. You yourself said so."

"There's no time to stroll down memory lane. I've got beautification to do. I need to shampoo and do my nails."

"And perhaps get dressed. What will you wear?"

"Black pants, white blouse, and my blue denim vest."

"Good. Denim takes years off," he says, stroking the hip pocket of his blue jeans.

"This girl probably wants to know how to get gigs in cabarets and music halls. In the fifties and sixties, being black, American, and female was an advantage here, but times have changed. Black American girls have it tougher these days. Those long, lean African girls—strutting up and down the *haute couture* runways—they're more in demand than the black Americans."

"If she is a dancer, one wants only to see that she is a good dancer."

"I sure hope she can sing, too. She needs to be super talented."

"You are lighting the filter tip of your cigarette, Violetta. You are on edge. Why?"

Putting out the wrong end of the cigarette, I realize I am on edge. "According to Odile, the girl looks like me and thinks I'm related to her. Wouldn't that put you on edge? Besides, I don't want to see anyone from the States just now. Later, when I'm in better shape."

"But you talk always about contacting relatives."

"By mail or talking on the phone. I'm not at my best, not in any condition right now to see or be seen by anybody. I don't feel like meeting a stranger. By the way, what do I owe you for the polish and stuff?"

"Do not worry about a few euros. Let me know if the girl wants a manager."

Before I can thank him, Jean-Louis and Boris are out the door on their way downstairs. I owe him more than a few euros. Money-wise he helps both me and one of his sisters, and manages to keep up appearances—keeps himself well dressed and well entertained. But his little nest egg has got to be shrinking. Soon we'll have only his government pension and mine to live on.

***

I go across to the café early. At three forty-five, I'm sitting at a table inside where it's cool. I put my cane on a chair at a nearby table, so it looks like somebody else left it there. The four guys at the bar are regulars, here every afternoon, on stools side-by-side like birds on a telephone wire. I blow a kiss to André the bartender, and ask for a Coke Light. I'd love to have a whiskey, but I can't. Doctor's orders. Besides, I need a clear head.

The café is a laid-back neighborhood spot, renovated a few years ago. The place was stripped bare to stone walls and exposed wooden beams. It's been decorated with old-fashioned posters: naked blonds advertising champagne and men wearing *chapeaux melons* and holding beer mugs. The mirrored bar reflects an array of bottles and stem glasses hanging from an overhead rack. The color scheme is mostly maroon. The owner's wife—she decorated the place—calls the color "claret." The "claret" carpet has the musty smell of a wine cellar. A TV set at one end of the bar entertains the regulars. André serves drinks. In the kitchen, Maurice makes a hefty *sandwich jambon* and a tasty *croque monsieur*.

André brings the Coke. I sip it and check my watch from time to time. It's almost four-fifteen when a taxi pulls up and out steps Odile. Behind her is a beautiful, brown, leggy doll of a girl. They look chic, both wearing all black—tight pants and T-shirts and, of course, sunglasses—although it's cloudy. Odile's friend has gold hoop earrings and natural hair in a boyish cut. When they come in, Odile leading the

34

way, the barflies eyeball them. Odile bends over and kisses my cheeks, then says, "This is Greta."

Greta removes her sunglasses. She has a skeptical expression, doubting dark eyes, and a half smile of disbelief. Just as Odile said, she looks the way I used to look: smooth, radiant copper-brown skin, high cheekbones, pert nub of a nose, long neck and collar bones that show—the way mine used to. I lift my chin, straighten my spine, throw back my shoulders, and suck in my gut. I'm trying to appear proud of the leftovers of my good looks, but how I envy her youth and natural beauty.

She leans over and firmly shakes my hand. "Violetta Mae Garfield aka Violet Fields from Louisville?" she asks.

"The one and only," I say coolly, but my heart is beating double time. She sure looks like a Garfield.

Her face brightens. She lets out a long sigh, as if she's been holding her breath from the moment she laid eyes on me. "I'm Hope, Aunt Violet!"

Somehow I get to my feet and hug her. Her light, floral fragrance blends with my spicy perfume. "Bless be the ties that bind," I hear myself say out loud. Odile's camera flashes, taking snapshots of our embrace. The guys at the bar turn to take it in.

"I wanted to surprise you," Odile says.

"The name Greta sure threw me off."

"I call myself Greta Grayson. I like the alliteration," Hope says.

I want to ask what she means by "a literation." Instead, I say, "Hope's a lovely name, but I changed mine, too. So I can't fault you for changing yours." I sit down and collect myself. Hope slides onto the chair facing me.

"A few days ago, I spoke of trying to find you and Faith. Talked about the last time I saw you."

"At Daddy's funeral."

"Yes, fifteen years ago. How you sang that day!"

I feel uneasy, wondering what Hope remembers about me, and what she has heard about me from her mother. What does she want? I wish she'd come years ago when I was in good form. But here we are, thrown together by that mischievous Odile. We try to size each other up, without being too obvious. She looks healthy, well cared for: perfect makeup, expensive sandals, professional pedicure. Her eyes soften as she looks at me. I'm sure she finds me much older and more ordinary than she'd expected.

Odile, still snapping pictures, says, "I wish I could stay, but I have a rendezvous with a producer for work in television commercials."

"Stay a while," I call out to Odile.

"Sorry, I ought not be late. I must go." She slips her camera into her backpack, quickly kisses us, and heads for the door. Leaving the café, she turns and waves.

Hope looks around, surveying the place. I'm in here every day, so it doesn't seem special. But she's looking around like she's in a museum. Or maybe she's just tense about our being alone.

Then, turning to me, she says, "I've tried to imagine how we'd meet. I've been excited about finding you." She sounds sincere.

"Well, you've found me." Something sweeps over me suddenly like a warm rush of air. My heart's beating like it's going to jump out of my bra.

"I started my search for you from Atlanta. Mom said she'd misplaced your address and phone number. So I called Paris Information for your number, but it's unlisted."

"Yeah, my husband, Stanley, had the number unlisted. We had to go *liste rouge*. We were getting lots of nuisance calls."

"I contacted record companies. They were no help. I telephoned the American Embassy, spoke to several agents. They told me you weren't registered and probably were no longer in France. So I decided to come over. I asked for you at some jazz clubs. Then I met Odile. When we had lunch last week, I mentioned trying to find my aunt, Violet Fields."

"I was puzzled when Odile said she'd met a Greta, a dancer from Atlanta, who might be related to me. If she'd said Louisville, I'd have thought it was likely. When did you go to Atlanta?"

"When I went to Spelman College. After I graduated, I stayed in Atlanta." I don't hear Louisville or Atlanta in her voice. She's got a crisp, educated accent like American TV anchors. And she talks fast.

"Did you go to college to study dance?" I'm wondering if Marie would have allowed that.

"I took a dance class in my senior year—just for fun—and loved it. And I sang in the Spelman choir, did some solos. After college, I did office work, waitressing, and modeling to pay for dance classes. I got a job at the Center for Dance Education of the Atlanta Ballet where I took lessons."

"Ballet lessons?"

"No, modern and jazz dance with Greta Altman, a terrific teacher. I liked her so much that I borrowed her name when I left Atlanta."

"So you've become Greta recently?"

"A couple of months ago. I'm not sure the name fits, but I kind of like it. When did you change your name?"

"Oh, years ago. A producer of New Faces 1952 said I needed a shorter name, more artsy than

37

Violetta Garfield. I suggested Violet Fields. He liked the name and it's stuck."

André comes to our table to take our order. "This is my niece from the States. André, I want you to meet..." I'm hesitating.

"Greta," she says briskly. "And I'll have a Perrier." Her glance lingers on his face, taking in his good looks. André is a beautiful blend of his French mother and Nigerian father. With his short dreadlocks and round, gold-rimmed glasses, he could pass for a Left Bank intellectual.

"Another Coke Light, Madame Violet?" And he's got good manners.

"Yes, please, André." I pause as he walks away, thinking Hope might say he's cute or something, but she doesn't. "Do you get to Louisville often?" I ask. We're eyeing each other cagily, as if we are reluctant to return to places where my question could lead.

"Two or three times a year."

"Marie, how is she? Do you have any snapshots of her?"

"She's fine. I didn't bring any recent pictures. I wish I had." From a black faux Prada bag, she hands me two photos: a publicity color portrait of me copied from a CD cover and a faded black-and-white snapshot of the three of us—Hampton, Marie, and me—as kids.

It's a close-up, head to waist of Hampton and me, and only head and shoulders of Marie. I turn it over to find in Mama's handwriting: "My children in 1946." I study our faces: mine at age fourteen; Hampton's going on thirteen, and three-year-old Marie's. I'd faked a smile. Hampton's open face, earnest eyes, and innocent smile were genuine. Childhood memories bubble up in me like an eruption of a volcano.

Hampton was a clever, horse-crazy kid, happiest when he came home with muck all over his sneakers. And he was smart—knew all there was to know about racehorses. He had big dreams about owning horses, standing in the winner's circle at the Kentucky Derby. No more than ten years old, he'd hold up a coffee can, pretending it was the Derby trophy cup, and make a little speech about his horse and his jockey.

Marie and I slept in the same room, Hampton on a cot downstairs. He'd come up in the middle of the night, wake me up to tell me about his dreams. For months he had the same dream: "Violetta Mae, you're decked out in a fine dress and fancy hat, singing 'The Star Spangled Banner' at the Kentucky Derby. Me, I'm in the race, a jockey trailing the pack, then gaining on them and driving ahead to win on my horse, Captain Marvel. In the winner's circle, I'm the jockey, the trainer, and the owner—all three." The dream always made me want to laugh, but I pretended to be annoyed. "Don't have me singing no national anthem. I don't like the tune or the words. Go back to bed and let me get some sleep." For a long time I'd lie awake, smiling in the dark, wishing Hampton's dream could come true.

Hampton and I were close. I guess I didn't feel close to Marie because I was her night and day baby-sitter. Sometimes I thought Mama had her to let me know what it takes to care for a kid, so I wouldn't get knocked up and have a baby myself. Caring for Marie robbed me of playtime, stole my childhood.

***

The snapshot holds my gaze as I relive the misery of taking care of Marie. Hope reaches for the picture and I return it to her. Pulling me out of the past, Hope says, "Mom remarried five years ago. She married Daddy's friend, Bill Knox, just a year after his wife died. She sold our house, moved in with him. They have a huge, new house in a suburban development." She tries to look blasé, but I hear a quiver in her voice that tells me she's not happy about the marriage or the move.

"I remember Billy Knox. Working at Churchill Downs, he knew how to hustle. Probably made good money."

"He's retired from the track. And Mom's retired from teaching. He and Mom play golf, follow the races, vacation on Martha's Vineyard."

"So Marie's got herself a nice life. Good for her." I notice I don't feel at all jealous. I'm really happy for her.

"And they visit his kids, his son in Santa Fe and his daughter in Los Angeles." Her long lashes blink back tears. "When I go to Louisville, I don't feel at home in their place. I usually stay with Daddy's sister, Margaret, or at a friend's place." She stares at the floor.

The place where my maternal urges live, just under my rib cage, is throbbing. I reach out with both hands, my blue fingernails and six silver rings—three on each hand—hands looking too tacky for what I'm feeling. I clasp her hands, clear nails and no rings, in mine.

"I'm sorry to get so upset, so emotional, Aunt Violet."

"Just call me Violet. Do you want me to call you Hope or Greta?"

"Call me Hope."

As André returns with the drinks, I'm telling Hope about the last time I saw her and heard her sing the sweetest "Amazing Grace" I'd ever heard.

"You had a good voice—a kid's voice, but with a lot of promise. I knew you could become a singer."

Hope says, "I want to combine dancing and singing. You've done both. That photo of you in the pale blue gown that sparkled with sequins—I used to sleep with it under my pillow. Mom had a scrapbook of articles about you, programs, and pictures. I looked at it almost every day."

"Oh?" I whisper, raising my eyebrows, surprised that Marie took some pride in my work.

She notices my expression and runs her fingers nervously around her closely cropped head, as if through hair that's no longer there.

"Whatever happened at the funeral put a lot of distance between you and Mom, but she tried to follow your career. After a while, there were fewer articles about you, and then you dropped out of the news. She worried about you, wondered what had happened to you."

"At the funeral, Marie said she didn't want me to visit again. So I said, OK, I wouldn't bother her. Flying there to be with her was expensive. I'd canceled a gig. It was a sacrifice. And frankly, she seemed more concerned about me attracting attention than grieving for your daddy. I know she was disturbed, but she was disrespectful. All the time I'd cared for her when she was a baby and a sickly child should have earned me some respect."

***

At first it was fun to play with Marie, a living doll to dress and push around West Louisville in the hand-me-down carriage that had been mine and then Hampton's. Hampton and me—we'd take turns pushing the carriage and pretend we were the parents. I put on a stern face like Mama's. Hampton had one of Papa's pipes between his lips to make him look grown-up. After a while, it wasn't a game. Caring for Marie became a chore. She doesn't know how much I did for her.

***

"Mom respects you. She said leaving Louisville and moving to Paris was brave and ambitious."

"Does she know you're here seeing me?"

André turns on the TV set above the bar to a rugby match. The stadium crowd is chanting. Groans and cheers from the fans at the bar follow the ball up and down the field. I lean toward Hope with my good ear. She notices and speaks louder.

"I told her I was coming to Paris and that I'd find you."

"I'm glad you did. Tell me about Faith."

"She went to college at Ohio State and stayed on there. She teaches math in a Cleveland high school. Last year she married Stuart Greenberg. They live in Shaker Heights with their golden retriever."

I get the feeling she and Faith aren't close and wonder if trouble between sisters is being visited on another generation. "Where were they married?"

"In Louisville."

"Was it a big wedding?"

"It was huge. Mom maxed out her credit cards for it. Faith's gown was fabulous. I was the maid of honor. Three bridesmaids. The reception was under a big tent at Bill and Mom's house. Beautiful food, a band, and dancing. It was awesome."

"Did his family attend?"

She nods. "His parents, grandmother, his two brothers, several cousins, and his friends."

If I'd been on good terms with Marie, she might've invited me. I love weddings. "Greenberg? How'd that go down with Marie?"

"Mom likes him a lot. Everybody got along well at the wedding." Realizing where my question is coming from, she says, "Attitudes are changing, at least on the surface, even in Louisville."

An elderly couple comes in, regulars who live in the *quartier*. They take a table near us.

"Any regrets about leaving Atlanta?"

"No. My job at the Arts Center was eliminated in June. The man I was seeing was pressuring me to get married. He's divorced, with custody of his two sons. I'm not ready to be a stepmother—or a mother. So it was a good time to get away."

"You'll have better offers." After a long silence, I ask, "Have you thought about the cost of living here? How long can you stay if you don't find work?" She needs to know now that she hasn't found a big-hearted aunt with a big, fat purse.

"I put the money Mom gave me in a savings account, my share from the sale of the house. So I have enough to live on for a while."

I'm trying to guess at the number of weeks she's calling "a while," when André comes over to the couple and takes their order: Pernod for him and Dubonnet for her. Hope glances at André as he walks back to the bar.

"Where are you staying?" I ask.

"I'm caretaking an apartment on rue Gay-Lussac in the fifth arrondissement. The family is in Norway for a month. I walk their dogs and water the plants. They come back the end of August, so in two weeks I have to move somewhere else." Her voice weakens and trails off. Sounding more confident, she says, "I know I'll find something. I always land on my feet."

"Speaking of landing on your feet, have you danced professionally?"

"In Atlanta I was in modern dance shows, doing jazz style, hip-hop, and tap. I've got a video of one of my performances. I'd love for you to see it. And I want to see films or videos of you dancing. Are there any videos of your shows?"

"I've got a video of my last Paris show with a big band. That was a few years back. We'll watch it sometime, if I can lay my hands on it. The last number, a Beatles tune, I sang in French, "Je Veux Prendre Ta Main," and then in English, "I Want to Hold Your Hand." Four guys—good dancers—dressed like the Beatles did a dance number with me. The crowd clapped the entire time, and we kept on dancing. I've got it on tape somewhere. It's been years since I looked at it."

On the edge of her seat, she says, "Mom said you performed all over Europe and in the Middle East. After Daddy's funeral she said you flew to Morocco for a show."

"Yes, that was my heyday."

"I remember you wore a mink stole and diamond rings at the funeral."

"I've traded diamonds for silver." I spread my fingers on the table and look at my rings with regret that I had to pawn my diamonds. I'd bought the fur stole just for the trip. I wanted everybody to think I'd made it big. I bragged about Stanley and his gigs, dropped names of famous bandleaders like they were close friends. I lied a little about how we were living. I wanted Marie to think show biz had paid off for me.

"Mom and her friends used to talk about you all the time. They said your husband—Faith and I called him Uncle Stanley, although we never knew him— played with the Count Basie Band. That you owned a Rolls Royce, had a chauffeur and a maid and a swimming pool. The family called you the next Josephine Baker."

This takes me aback. So Marie boasted about me. Could she really have classed me with Josephine?

"I was never near her level. You have no idea how grand Josephine Baker was." I'm quiet for a moment, thinking of Josephine's life and mine. "My life has been humdrum by comparison. I had some lucky breaks—cabaret runs, gigs in good clubs, parts in musicals, cut some albums, had a few foreign trips. But nothing that comes close to her success. Her lifestyle was truly glamorous."

"You had a glamorous lifestyle, too. At least, what you've done seems glamorous to me."

"Glamorous? There are tricks that make you look glamorous. Good camera work can cut out a tacky background. Costumes and wigs change your looks. And you pose beside other people's cars, boats, and swimming pools. To get gigs and fans, you have to squeeze into borrowed gowns, lay on the makeup, and look like you live on Easy Street.

"I wanted to impress your mom and the Louisville crowd, but I don't want to fool you. I live alone in a second story walk-up apartment across the street in this honky-tonk, red light district. Lived here with Stanley until he died two years ago. Before that we lived in cheap hotels. Glamorous? Hell, no, but we made it sound glamorous. You need to know show biz is all surface." I'm not sure she's getting the point, so I say, "It's tough being an entertainer in Paris. What else do you know how to do?"

"I was a history major at Spelman."

"In the States you could teach history."

"Teach history, marry some guy, live in the suburbs, and walk my golden retriever? No thanks, that's not for me."

"You're here walking dogs for strangers. Where's that going to get you?"

"I'm also auditioning for shows and looking for other work at restaurants and modeling agencies. I was hired to model last night for a life-drawing class. I didn't like it at all. I'd rather work with clothes on, maybe do fashion modeling." Again she nervously runs her fingers over her brush cut.

"By the way, how's your French?" I'm not letting up. She needs to know what it takes to make a go of things here.

"*Je lis et comprends bien, et chaque jour je parle mieux, c'est-à-dire, plus clairement,*" she says with an American accent.

"Where'd you learn such good French?"

"I started French in seventh grade and continued through college."

"Well, you just might make it. Odile told me you want a mentor. What's that all about?"

"I need someone with experience to tell me how to get jobs in clubs and music halls. How to get an agent or manager, that sort of thing." She looks eager, lifting her chin, stretching her neck, moving her shoulders, like she's about to audition for me.

She reminds me of how eager and raring to go I was at her age. I didn't have a mentor, agent, or manager. I auditioned constantly, even when I had work. When I didn't have a gig, I took whatever job kept me on the scene—worked in the box office or backstage, helped with costumes and makeup. If I couldn't get cabaret or club work, I did sewing and baby-sitting for girls who were working. Altogether I put in more nights backstage than onstage.

"If you want my advice, try to hook up with a talented, high-powered French manager. If he's available and you like him, marry him so he'll have a stake in promoting you. Foreign women who make it big here are all married to Frenchmen in entertainment."

She says coolly, "I want to build a career before getting involved."

"I don't know how I can help. I don't have the contacts I used to. The scene's changed a lot recently. Fewer clubs, not many big shows with chorus lines. But, OK, I'll speak with Jean-Louis Duval. He used to be my manager. We'll find somebody to give you a start." To be honest, I don't know anybody in the business now, and neither does he. In my vagueness, I think she hears the truth of the matter.

"How did you get started here?"

"I came over from New York with New Faces 1952. After three weeks, the show folded. Most of the cast went back to the States, but I knew I wanted to stay. I felt at home here, at ease with myself, comfortable in my skin. I'd been made to feel more foreign in Louisville than I ever have here."

"Can you lay out the chronology of your Paris career?" Ready to take notes, Hope pulls out a pen and spiral notebook.

"I've got no chronology—whatever that is. So put away that notebook. I can tell you about some great and not-so-great gigs, some high times and hard times. In the beginning there was Josephine Baker. I bet a lot of colored girls were like me—saw her pictures and dreamed of being glamorous like her. Pretending I was Josephine, I'd sing along with vocalists on the radio. I always wanted to be onstage, singing and dancing.

"When I was sixteen, I fell for a horse trainer, Pierre Prince from Martinique. He was in Louisville for the races. The first time I heard French was from him. At the end of the Churchill Downs season, he asked me to go to Saratoga, New York, with him. I quit school, left after eleventh grade at Central High. I told Mama and Papa I was going north for a summer job. They made a big fuss, but they didn't stop me because I told them I'd make some money and send money home. And I said I'd come back to finish school. I got work as a waitress in a Saratoga nightclub. Made good money that summer. When the Saratoga season ended, Pierre told me he was married and was returning to Martinique to his wife and children. I was heartbroken."

Remembering just how coldly he said it, real casual while he was packing his bags, still makes me shudder.

"What did you do then?"

"In Saratoga, I'd met a talented dancer, Mable Henderson, who was from Louisville. She took me under her wing. She told me to forget Pierre and go to New York with her. Went in the fall of 1948. I suppose I don't need to tell you what that time was like for Negroes—even in New York. I got a lucky break. Joined the cast of New Faces 1952. Like I told you, the show folded here—but I didn't fold."

"So how did you get started here?"

"I'll tell you all about that later, when I can show you what I'm going to put in my picture albums and scrapbooks, when I organize all that stuff."

"I'd like to help you with that." She seems genuinely interested in me. Almost too interested.

"Before I can get to the album and scrapbooks, there's a lot of work to do at my place. You know, in Paris, people don't ask you into their homes right away. I've become Parisian in that respect." I'm trying to buy some time, put off the day she sees me *chez moi.*

She moves our empty glasses aside. Reaching across the table for my hand, she says, "You remember how we lived in Louisville, so you don't need to be ashamed of your place."

My mind takes a trip back to the kitchen of the tiny shotgun house where Hampton and I played checkers and cards on the kitchen table under a bare light bulb. Too young for our games, Marie sat on the kitchen floor looking up at the TV. One day she was watching some dumb white family program. I think it was Leave It to Beaver. Hampton stopped our card game and said, "I don't think Negroes can have a house and stuff like that. Houses you see on TV cost big money. And I don't see no way of making big money."

When I went to Lloyd's funeral, I saw that Marie and he had improved the house some: put on aluminum siding, built a front porch, and added two rooms. But it was still a shabby house on a shabby street in a shabby part of town.

"Marie was smart to sell that house," I tell Hope. "You wouldn't want to live there, would you?"

She shakes her head and whispers, "No, but I don't know where I do want to live."

"If you're thinking of living in Paris, you need to find steady work."

Glancing at her watch, she gasps. "Sorry, but I've got to go and walk the dogs. When can I see you again?" She flashes the Garfield smile—lips stretched wide, showing the gap between her front teeth.

"Phone me sometime," I say, hoping she'll wait a few days before calling. I need time to prepare for our getting better acquainted.

She jots down her number in the notebook, tears out the page, and gives it to me. I tell her mine. She scribbles my phone number and under it prints, "Aunt Violet."

She puts a ten-euro note on the table. I push it toward her, shaking my head. "This is on me. When you get work, then you can pay." I nod to André, who comes to our table. He says to Hope, "Come in again," and bows slightly. She smiles in his direction but doesn't say a word. She's cool.

I stand up and feel unsteady. There's that numbness in my feet. I look around, see my cane, but don't reach for it. She kisses my cheeks in the French manner. "*À trés bientôt*," she says with a big smile. Her fragrance, *muguet*, lingers. I hobble to the door to watch her step into the early evening parade of buyers, sellers, and gawkers. I'm thinking, that's my niece. She's got some of what it takes—great looks, talent, youth, and brains. But I wonder if she has the drive and confidence you need to make it in Paris today? I hate to think of what my chances would be if I were starting out now—alone, with no Stanley to guide me.

Paris is a fickle teacher, especially if you're training for the entertainment scene. One day she makes you feel you're the best student in the class, and the very next day she sits you in a corner, a dunce cap on your head. Paris, be gentle. Be kind to Hope.

7

That night I dreamed I had a daughter, a pretty little girl, six or seven years old. Walking in the Luxembourg Garden, I was holding her hand. Suddenly she was an adult and not my daughter at all. She'd become Hope. I dropped her hand and ran. The feeling of running woke me.

Sitting up in bed, I saw Josephine, looking young, with a blue spotlight on her face. In her girlish, tinkling voice, she sang a few bars: "Climb up on my knee, Sonny Boy..." It was nice to see her looking cheerful and sounding young. She spoke, called me by name, and said, "Violet, she's kin. Give her a helping hand. Take her under your wing." The blue light surrounding her swirled into an aura encircling Josephine's face. Then she disappeared and the light faded away.

"How can I help Hope? Does she need to know about the down-and-out times? Or should I tell her only about the lucky breaks, the good gigs? I don't want to discourage her, but I've got to be honest," I said to the fading light.

***

I need to get a move on, get out of my nightie and into something decent. Jean-Louis and Boris will be here soon. But instead of getting dressed, I visit Stanley's pictures. After that, I shuffle into the dining room and start sorting the loose photos stored in shoeboxes. Pictures of me in sequined gowns sitting on the laps of horny studs at cabarets, putting on makeup at a backstage dressing room mirror, cavorting in scanty costumes with gals whose names I can't recall, dancing cheek to cheek with Stanley, posing in a bikini on the beach at Cannes, taking a bow with a bouquet of flowers.

A photo of Stanley and me at a Paris civil rights rally in August '63 brings back memories. We couldn't afford to go to the States for the March on Washington, so we went to the rally in support of the March at the American Cathedral. There was a huge gathering of writers, artists, actors, musicians, celebrities, and students—black and white. The pews were filled when we arrived, so Stanley and I found standing room in the back. People overflowed onto Avenue George V. Kisses and greetings were tossed here and there. Waiting for the program to begin, somebody shouted, "Freedom now!" In response another voice cried, "*Liberté, egalité. fraternité!*" The crowd began a chant with both slogans. It was a grand show of solidarity; but when I looked around I saw who wasn't chanting—who'd been planted among us in the service of the CIA. Agents and informants, black and white, male and female were there—some of the same faces I'd seen in the cafés and restaurants we frequented. I nudged Stanley and nodded in the direction of guys we nicknamed Amos and Andy. "The noble nigger spies," Stanley said. "Look at the ratio. They've got at least one agent for every person here."

The program started with speeches about racism in the States and the courage and patience of black Americans. One speaker urged blacks in the crowd to go back to the States, become part of the solution. I felt guilty for not being political, not being a part of the movement. Just before this picture was taken, I'd said to Stanley, "Let's go back, move to Harlem, and get involved." The photographer caught him scowling. Stanley was saying, "Hell, no. You can go if you want. But I've got nothing to gain by going back—and neither do you. Why struggle for the hope of decency and respect in the States when you're living it here and now?" Later I thought about what he said, weighed what I had to gain and lose. I knew my skin color made a difference here; but it was in my favor. Being an American Negro in Paris at that time drew interest and sympathy. It was a benefit in Paris, a bonus. Besides, I had regular work, an album in production, an apartment, and my man. Stanley was right. I knew for sure then that I would stay in Paris, hand over my US passport, and become a French citizen.

Ours was a show-biz marriage, one or both of us occasionally on tour. We spent days, sometimes weeks, apart. At first, Stanley had much more work than I did. He was older and had a reputation. I was often alone and lonely, and maybe a little jealous. I always worried that he might fall for somebody else. After Jean-Louis took me on, I got good gigs with contracts. But Stanley's career and mine were still out of sync. When my scene was hot, his seemed to cool down.

I wish we'd taken snapshots of the everyday, down-to-earth side of our lives: Stanley taking pleasure in a breakfast of bacon, sunny-side up eggs, and hash brown potatoes at the kitchen table; Stanley in his robe and slippers and me in my red kimono in the living room listening to tapes; Stanley asking what I thought of this or that riff. In ordinary times, it was a laid-back, ordinary marriage. But when one of us had the spotlight totally, those demons of marriage—envy and jealousy—came between us. Now I regret the resentment I felt and things I did and said out of spite. Sometimes I told Stanley I was sorry, but I wish I'd told him more often.

I find more pictures and more memories in plastic bags and shoeboxes. I don't know when or where most were taken. A couple of hours have passed, and I'm still sorting photos and selecting memories, harking back to days when I was hoofing and crooning and mostly happy doing it.

A knock at the door. Jean-Louis is here and I'm not dressed. "*J'arrive, Jean-Louis, j'arrive. Patience.*" A glance in the mirror tells me I don't even want Jean-Louis to find me looking like this. Anyhow, I open the door.

"Monique! What are you doing here? I was expecting Jean-Louis."

"*Bonjour*, Violet. I am taking my cousin to the zoo, and I thought you might like to go. We can wait, if you want to go."

"No, thank you, it would take me too long to get dressed. Besides, I've got to start a major cleanup here. Getting things organized."

"After the zoo trip, I can return to help you."

Lord knows I need help, but I hesitate, not knowing what I can ask her to do. Saved by the howl Boris sends up, I say, "That must be Boris with Jean-Louis. He's come to help."

"Telephone if you need me." On the way down, Monique has some soothing French words for Boris, who slinks past her into the apartment. She and Jean-Louis exchange greetings and kisses on the stairs.

"Violetta, it is noon and still you are *déshabillée*," Jean-Louis says looking me up and down. "Are you going well?"

"I've got a lot on my mind and I'm not myself."

"You look depressive. Why are you not yourself?"

"I'm an aunt. My niece, Hope, is in Paris. I met her yesterday. The Greta I was going to meet, she's actually my niece, Marie's younger daughter."

"Your niece is in Paris? *Félicitations!* Is she a nice girl?"

"Come on in. I'll tell you about her."

Jean-Louis follows my halting steps and the tap of my cane into the living room. He moves the plastic laundry basket, overflowing with dirty clothes, from the leather lounge chair to the floor and takes a seat. Easing into the straight-back chair opposite, I'm wearing my serious face. "She's got a college education, good legs, and good French."

"And her looks?"

"She's my color—a copper brown with cheekbones showing the Cherokee in her. Large eyes that look surprised, snub nose, broad smile. Natural looking makeup. Mature voice. Her hair's cut real short. Dressed in black, of course. She's slim, but she's got what Stanley called nice apples and pears. Great looks. She looks a lot like me when I was her age, but taller by three inches or more. Long legs. And she has the walk, walks like a model."

"Does she have personality, energy, stamina? That certain flair, that gleam in her eye? Can she sing? Can she dance? Dance like Josephine?"

"What are you thinking?"

Jean-Louis lifts his eyebrows and flutters his lashes the way he does when he's flirting. "Ah, to find a girl fresh and daring and have her dazzle Paris like Josephine did. It would be fantastic!" He tosses his head back, closes his eyes, and whistles a few bars of "J'ai Deux Amours." Then he says, "Paris is ready for another Josephine. There is a grand nostalgia for her style, her image. One finds her on posters and postcards everywhere. The advertisers use her in fashion scenes. I saw a huge billboard with Josephine in Gare d'Austerlitz promoting rail travel to see the Dordogne and Josephine's chateau. Paris still loves her. Your niece could be transformed, made over in Josephine's image!"

"A nice fantasy," I say coolly, trying to contain my own excitement about the idea.

"We can make what you call fantasy come true," he crows.

"We? Jean-Louis, we don't even know anybody in show business anymore. Let's face it; we've been out of it for years. Besides, the business is totally different now."

"I have some new contacts at the Métropole Theatre. It is reopening in November. Let me meet her and see what she can do."

"The Métropole will be the height of chic. You can't put on a skimpy production there. In a house like that, you've got to have *beaucoup* financial backing."

"I need only to find the talent. The money will follow. And it will not be skeempy." The old rooster is getting cocky. His chin is in the air, shoulders thrown back, tail feathers fluttering.

Twenty years ago, when Jean-Louis had an office and a secretary, he was a five-star manager and agent for a dozen acts. He knew all the old boys in show biz. He boasted that with no more than three phone calls, he could book us anywhere in Europe. One by one, the old boys began to drop out, retire, die. He doesn't have a clue now about contacts, and neither do I. The best I can do for Hope is to let my pictures tell the story of the business.

"She wants to come here and help me with my photos and scrapbooks. But we've got to get this place in some kind of order before she comes," I say, looking at the clutter.

"We? Not me. This place needs a professional cleaning service." His arms are stretched wide like a bandleader's, and with the wave for the downbeat, he repeats, "Professional!"

"Do you know a cleaning service?"

"I know a team that does theater sets. They know how to clean, arrange things artistically—and how to hide things. They work fast. How long is she in Paris?"

"Indefinitely."

"We have time then."

"No, she wants to visit me here—and soon. She may need a place to stay at the end of the month."

"She would want to stay here?" He looks first at the water-stained ceiling and then at the threadbare carpet. With a nod to the photographs around us, he adds, "Here with you—and Stanley?"

"Maybe so. I ought to take down some of these pictures. Get some nice frames and hang some photos of myself. What do you think?"

"Grand idea! I like it. *Alors,* tell me what you need from the market. I need to make the errands."

I get up and hobble to the kitchen. He and Boris are right behind me.

"Before going to bed last night, I jotted down some items," I say handing him a sheet of paper. Jean-Louis looks at the list. His jaw drops. I knew it would surprise him.

"These are foods you have to cook! A whole chicken, mushrooms, pearl onions, bacon, parsley, potatoes, and more. Violetta, you do not cook. Why should I get these?"

"I'm planning to cook her a fine French dinner—*coq au vin.*"

"Have you made *coq au vin* ever?

"No, never. But I've got an idea about how to do it. I've got a recipe for it in one of the magazines under the table in the dining room."

"Triage, please. First, we find a cleaning team. Two, we fix this place. Three, we advance to cooking," he says counting off with his skinny fingers.

I add, "And we get Hope work in a revue or a club. We've got lots to do!" My head is buzzing with lists and ideas. I'm having a surge of energy that feels like 220 volts. It feels good.

8

The next morning at nine o'clock, Jean-Louis phones and says, in his bossy tone, "I have hired a team to make over your apartment. They will arrive after lunch at three. They have their instructions. You need only to let them in and stay out of their way." He hangs up before I can protest.

I'm not crazy about the idea of strangers with stage set ideas fixing up my place. So I start in the bedroom, dusting here and there, changing the sheets, hanging up clothes, putting hats and shoes in boxes, and so on. I try on dresses I haven't worn for years. The chartreuse chiffon gown I wore in my last show still fits, but barely. Anyway it feels good to be in costume again. In the bathroom, I put on the makeup that goes with the gown, green eye shadow and all.

As the clock of Eglise St-Pierre strikes three, someone knocks at my door. I open it and find three mustached, middle-aged Frenchmen in blue work coats. The tallest is carrying a ladder and a radio-cassette player. Behind him is a fellow of medium height, holding a pail of sponges, rags, and detergents in one hand and, in the other, two feather dusters, a broom, and a mop. The shortest, a bald, child-sized man, not quite a midget, struggles under the weight of a vacuum cleaner. The little man's rich basso profundo startles me when he bellows, "*Bonjour, Madame. Nous sommes les amis de Jean-Louis. Je m'appelle Monsieur Petit, et mes colleagues sont Monsieur Midi et Monsieur Legrand.*"

"*Entrez,*" I say as they troop in and place their paraphernalia in the foyer. Legrand looks at me, with an expression that asks, why is Madame wearing an evening gown in the afternoon? He strides along the hall, surveying the space from floor to ceiling. The others follow him. I'm a few steps behind. From time to time, Midi mutters, "*Mon Dieu,*" obviously disturbed by the condition of the place. They inspect each room, including the bathroom and kitchen, turning lights on and off as they go. I can't understand much of their whispered, rapid-fire French slang. I gather they will paint some walls and wash windows. Petit makes a list: three lamps, light bulbs, red paint, bolts of velour, meters of muslin, plastic stools, two large palm plants, and a lemon tree. Leaving to do the errands, Petit calls out to his partners, "*Courage!*"

Midi turns to me and says in a polite manner, "*Madame, s'il vous plait, mettez les robes dans l'amoire.*"

I smile. I've spent the morning stuffing clothes in the armoires. They won't hold any more.

"*Oui, bien sûr,*" I say, and go to the bedroom to deal with more clothes I no longer wear. I'll put them in suitcases and duffle bags that won't be traveling again.

Offenbach's "Can Can" music suddenly is blaring. Putting aside a bundle of scarves and feather boas, I shuffle into the living room to see what's going on. Midi and Legrand prance around like a pair of well-rehearsed acrobats, rolling up the carpet, taking down draperies, throwing open shutters, and whisking cobwebs away with feather dusters. They pause, exchange a few words, and whirl into action again.

Petit returns with paint and bundles of fabric. He leaves them in the foyer and announces he's now going to buy plants. I offer him euros. He refuses them, telling me that Jean-Louis is paying for everything.

I know Jean-Louis has been disturbed because I haven't kept up the place since Stanley died. Such a prissy old maid, that Jean-Louis. His apartment is super neat—impeccable, he insists. But what have I done for him that compares to this mission of mercy? I listen to his show-biz anecdotes repeated over and over again, laugh or cry like I'm hearing them for the first time. I vouch for the accuracy of his memories about outrageous stuff, like the time Princess Grace telephoned him directly. He thought it was a hoax, so he cursed the caller and then hung up on her. Her secretary called back and explained that it was Princess Grace inviting him to organize the Monaco Red Cross benefit ball. We howl at least once a week about that one. He says it's healthy to be reminded of better times, when we knew everybody and everybody knew us. I guess I'm good for his spirits. I know he's good for mine.

What's that odor? Ammonia, bleach, lemon? They're going after the smells: sweaty shoes, spoiled food, Leo's litter box. I hear them moving my furniture around. Peeping out from the bedroom, I see they've taken down all of Stanley's pictures. Legrand sees I'm shocked. He explains that Jean-Louis said they were to be removed. He asks if I've got photos of myself to replace them.

Do I have pictures! I show him the boxes and stacks of photos in the dining room; and posters rolled up in a corner. He tells me to select some.

"No, it would take me forever," I tell him. "You can pick out the best." I look on for a while and see that he's choosing my favorites: several chorus line shots; me singing at the Lido in a black, strapless gown; crooning with Lena Horne in London; dancing with Geoffrey Holder; dining with Duke Ellington; skiing in the Alps; wearing a bikini in St. Tropez;

holding Stanley's arm in Moscow. Those were the days.

Cancan music is playing nonstop. Midi is mopping the floor and, at the same time, dancing the cancan, flapping his blue work coat like it's a skirt. I applaud and tell him I wish I could dance it with him.

Petit returns with potted palms that dwarf him. In French I explain that I'm no good at caring for plants because I have a brown thumb. He doesn't get it; it's one of those things you can't translate. Legrand tells him to place the plants in the dining room where they have covered my rickety chairs with off-white slip covers.

Petit tells them to wait until they see the huge lemon tree that's being delivered.

When they finish the floor in the living room, they vacuum the carpet. One threadbare patch is covered with a potted palm; the other is hidden under a cabinet. The mirror that was hanging vertically has been turned horizontally. Below the mirror, my tattered sofa is covered with crisp, ivory muslin. They've replaced my old, wooden coffee table with three—red, blue, and yellow—plastic stools. My CD player has been placed on a shelf. On the opposite wall they've hung an arrangement of photos of me in the silver and gold frames that had held Stanley's. With the draperies taken down and windows washed, the room is much brighter. It's almost prettified enough to be photographed for one of the slick, house-proud magazines.

They move their equipment into the bedroom. Leo springs out of his hiding place under the bed and takes cover somewhere else. Midi says they want to paint the cracked wall a color they call ruby. He shows me a paint chip. Brothel red is what the music-hall girls call it. I tell him I don't know if I can sleep with that color. Legrand, pointing to the corner table with pictures of Josephine, says, "Josephine Baker *a aimé beaucoup cette couleur.*"

"*Vraiment?*" I ask.

"*Oui*, Madame," he says with confidence. In that case, the color will be perfect, I tell him.

I point to Josephine's corner and advise, "*Ne touchez pas.*"

I'm famished. They scarcely notice when I say I'm going to the café across the street. One step at a time, I start downstairs, thinking that my place won't feel like home after the face-lift they're giving it. Face-lifts are deceiving, and they don't last. Sooner or later, the face begins to sag again.

As I cross the street, a taxi speeds by, almost knocking me over. I give the rear fender a whack with my cane. The driver sticks his fist out the window, gives me the finger, and shouts something that sounds like "*femme folle*" or crazy woman. I'm in the street in the afternoon wearing a long gown, feather boa wrapped around my neck, looking dazed. Maybe I am a little crazy.

Standing in the door of the café, André witnesses the scene. He crosses the street, takes my arm, and escorts me into the empty café. I'm sputtering about taxi drivers and fast traffic. He says, "*Calme. Doucement*, Madame Violet," as if pacifying a child. I'm grateful for his hand at my elbow, but his attitude is annoying. Without my asking, he brings me a Coke Light, what I would have ordered if he'd asked me. So why am I pissed off? Irritated and anxious about the way life is spinning around me, I feel I'm on a Ferris wheel I can't get off.

"*Ça va*, Madame Violet?"

"*Ça va, mais la vie est difficile aujourd'hui,* André."

In English, he asks in that same patronizing tone, "How can I be of help?"

"An invasion is in progress across the street. Jean-Louis has sent in his troops. They're occupying my apartment." I'm shaking a bit.

"I saw workmen go in. I talked with the short man. He said they're renovating your place. That's good."

"Good? I told you about the pictures of my husband all over the living room walls. Remember? Well, they've taken down Stanley's pictures, replaced them with pictures of me. I don't know what to tell Stanley."

André raises his thick, dark eyebrows, and says very slowly, "But your husband is dead, isn't he?"

"Yes, but I have something to say to his pictures nearly every day." I see he doesn't understand, just can't imagine me speaking to dead Stanley.

"I think your husband would want you to have your own photos on exhibit. And he'd be pleased about having the place fixed up. Now what else may I bring you?"

I almost forgot that I've come with a craving for a *croque-monsieur*. I order one, sip my Coke, and mull over what André just said. I guess Stanley would like me to display my pictures. And if the place looks better, I won't mind having people come in. I could have a little party for Hope at my place. And if I'm around next June, God willing, I could throw a birthday party for Josephine and myself. I've always wanted to have a combined celebration of her birthday and mine, which is the next day, June 4. Never had a birthday party when I was a kid. My folks didn't have the time or the money for parties.

Stanley wanted to have a party for me when I turned fifty; but I didn't want people to know my age then. Now it's different. With all the friends who've passed on, I feel lucky to be alive.

But what's the use of fixing up the place and changing my way of living if Old Man Trouble is just around the corner? It's a big expense for Jean-Louis. I don't know how it can make things better for me. Different, yes. But better? I don't know. It's all because of Hope. I wouldn't have had my life turned upside down if Hope hadn't come on the scene.

"*Croque monsieur, madame,*" André says and, with a flourish, puts the plate on the table. He lingers and polishes the table next to mine. It looks clean, not needing the vigorous wipe he's giving it. When I have a mouthful, he says, "When is your niece going to visit you again?"

So he noticed her. I signal that I'm chewing. Moments later I say, "She's coming tomorrow. I've invited her for dinner."

"It was good to see you two together—to know you have a relative here."

"Oh?" I'm surprised at André's interest in my situation.

"Are you renovating so she can live with you?"

"The place is getting a face-lift because it needs it. Besides, I think she wants to be on her own." At the same time, I'm thinking Hope and I could try living together for a few weeks, when she's between places. It might be good for me to have somebody else—other than Stanley, Leo, and Josephine—around me.

André greets a customer and goes to the bar to serve him. They exchange a few comments about the tennis match on television. André increases the volume. I turn around to watch the game just as the

Williams sister who's bleached her hair wins the set. I let out a cheer for her. I'm still clapping when Jean-Louis comes through the door.

"*Bonjour à tous*," he says with a nod toward the bar. Jean-Louis comes over to me with his big smirk and kisses my cheeks. I'm almost gassed by the lavender scent he's wearing. I need to tell him it's too heavy, thicker than the air in Provence. But this isn't the moment.

"Violetta, I hope you are happy with the new look *chez toi*?"

"You've gone to a lot of trouble and expense to..."

"No problem. They've nearly finished *le grand projet*. Let's go and congratulate them."

I find my cane and get up. Only then Jean-Louis notices what I'm wearing. "An evening gown in the afternoon?"

"It's a costume that goes with the theater set being installed in my pad." Limping toward the door, I take Jean-Louis' arm, and together we cross the street.

9

Sitting at the kitchen table without my eyeglasses, I'm holding a magazine at arm's length and reading aloud, "Two dozen pearl onions, ten medium-sized mushrooms, and..." I stop listing the ingredients for *coq au vin* and ask myself, "What if Hope doesn't eat chicken? She looks like she doesn't eat at all." Marie was finicky about food. Hope may be, too.

Marie. It's been so long since I've been in touch with her, I wouldn't know how to talk to her if she sat down at this table. If I phone her, I won't know what to say. I suppose I could begin by talking about Hope.

It took her and Lloyd some time to have Faith and Hope. Marie was forty or more when Faith was born; and he was over fifty. I wonder if she ever really loved Lloyd or if she married him because he was an experienced handyman and she wanted a family. Anyway, I'm glad she and Billy Knox have gotten together. Seems like he's giving her a better life. He's older, too, but not as old as Lloyd was. They should have some good years.

"The potatoes!" I get up from the table and get to the stove. Opening the oven door, the aroma of roasting potatoes blows by me, smelling good. Back at the table, I sit and continue reading the recipe, still thinking about Marie.

I'd always thought Marie disapproved of my kind of life. She seemed to look down on being in show business. With Hope following in my footsteps, I bet Marie is flipping out.

I'll ask Hope if I should call Marie. I can hear myself on the phone chattering about Hope and how well brought up she is, telling Marie it feels good to have her here to remind me of home. Marie may hang up—or throw up and then hang up.

Funny I should think about her throwing up. She threw up a lot when she was a kid. She was a skinny kid, skinny from birth. Weighed four pounds, Mama said. I started taking care of her when she was an infant. Mama handed her over to me when she went out to work. She worked at night; Papa worked days. The idea was there'd be somebody with us all the time. Papa generally came home late from the track. Many a time, it was just the three of us—little Marie, Hampton, and me—around the house in the evenings. She'd eat, then cry, then vomit—night after night. Even when she started school, she was doing the same thing. First they said she had ulcers. Later a doctor said it could be Crohn's disease, but they never found the real cause.

Sometimes it seemed like she threw up on purpose. Marie did it on my birthday, a warm June evening. Dressed up for a date with Pierre, I was looking fine in a tight black jersey blouse, pleated skirt with black polka dots on white, and high-heeled white pumps. Hampton was at the racetrack. Marie knew I was going to leave her alone for a while, but Hampton and Papa were coming home. Whimpering, she followed me to the door. I bent down to look into her face and tell her I'd be coming back soon. She let out a cry, and suddenly her supper of Franco-American macaroni rocketed out of her mouth and onto my skirt. That did it. I'd had enough of taking care of her—feeding and dressing her, giving her the medicines, walking her to and from school, helping with her schoolwork, putting her to bed. I had other household chores and my own schoolwork. I knew in that instant I was going to get out of that skirt, out of that house, and out of Louisville. The next night

Pierre asked me to go to Saratoga with him. Lord knows, I was more than ready.

When I went back to Louisville for my once-a-year visits that Christmas, I tried to talk to Marie. She wouldn't talk to me. I'd seen her talking to other folk. After a while I asked her, "Why aren't you talking to me?"

She hung her head and said, "Mama don't want me to catch the disease you got."

"What disease?"

"Mama said you're sick of Louisville and sick of us. And it's a bad disease."

After that, when I visited I kept my distance in case my condition was contagious, so Marie wouldn't get sick of Louisville.

***

Marie had just started college at Kentucky State University in Frankfort when Mama had a stroke and died. For the first time, Marie was living away from home. She came back to Louisville for the funeral. I flew over from Paris. Marie and two friends, Gloria and Tiffany, met me at the airport. Marie looked gaunt, haggard, and much older than eighteen. She's been orphaned, I thought, and I really felt for her. I put down my suitcases and wrapped my arms around her. Under a brown cable knit sweater, she felt skeletal—all skin and bones. She went limp on me and started crying. "I was afraid you wouldn't come. Mama's gone, and I don't have anyone now—no one but you."

Untangling my guilt, grief, affection, and resentment, I said, "Marie, I'm here for you, to take care of you."

"Promise to stay here and live with me. Promise?"

Gloria and Tiffany moved in close to pick up my bags and to hear me promise. They waited for me to say something. I was wishing Hampton would turn up, take over the situation, and release me from another round of duty.

Gently I eased Marie out of my arms and onto her feet. She was in a bad way. I was thinking maybe I should stay a while. I began calculating how to extend my visit beyond the week I'd planned. I could change my return ticket, call Stanley, and tell him I was needed in Louisville. It wasn't like I was in demand on the Paris scene at the time. Still, I needed to be there in case the gig of a lifetime turned up. Maybe I should stay and undo the job Mama had done on her, stunted her spirit with fear of the wrath of God. I'd make her take some risks, get a little more fun out of life—flirt, dance, party a little. Maybe I should stay a while.

"I can't promise to live here, Marie. My work, my home, my life—all that's in Paris. But I'll stay as long as I can." During the drive from the airport to our street, I asked Marie about funeral arrangements. None had been made. I asked about her plans. She had no plans. She was uncertain about whether to continue at the university. Her childish manner troubled me. She was frightened and confused. I wondered how she would manage on her own. Gloria, at the wheel, turned into our street. Parking in front of our house, she said, "There's no place like home, ma'am."

I stepped out of the car and looked up and down the street at its narrow, wood shingled houses—some abandoned and boarded up, others recently painted, expanded, and protected from burglars with iron grillwork on windows. At our house there were new steps and a railing. Improvements were underway. I

70

felt I was seeing a television program about changes in a Negro neighborhood in America's south. It seemed far away and foreign. I knew then I wasn't going to live in Louisville ever again.

Every time the phone rang or somebody knocked on the door, I hoped it might be Hampton. I needed his help. I wanted Marie to make some choices about selection of the casket, pallbearers, music, and eulogies for the service. She looked to me to handle all the funeral arrangements, the insurance agent, and the grasping cousins who came to make off with Mama's things. I told her, "Keep all the furnishings. And you can have the house." I didn't want to get tied up in legal paperwork for a little piece of property I had no use for. She was happy to know the place would still be her home. She was thinking of getting a job in Louisville instead of returning to school. "Rent the house, go back to that college, and get a teacher's degree. That's what Mama would want you to do," I said.

I ended up staying two weeks in Louisville, hoping, in vain, for word from Hampton. The night before I left, the deaconesses from Mama's church, in their white uniforms and black gloves, came to the house to pray for us. They called us Sister Marie and Sister Violetta Mae in their churchy style. I realized I'd never felt sisterly toward Marie. When we were young, we'd never shared children's games, neighborhood adventures, or family secrets. The difference in our ages separated us; besides, I was more her caretaker than her sister. After the deaconesses left, I hugged Marie, kissed her, and told her, "We have to learn to love each other like sisters. You're my only close kin and I'm yours." Somehow I couldn't keep hold of the closeness I felt for Marie at that moment in Louisville. And she couldn't hold on to that feeling for me.

With no contact with Marie for some time, I can't compare what's going on inside me with what's happening to somebody of the same flesh and blood. I wonder if Marie's diabetic, if she has dizzy spells and blurred vision, if her feet get numb? Does she have high blood pressure? Is she arthritic? Is her hair thinning? Are her gums softening? Do spirits visit her, too? I wonder if she's becoming anything like me?

A knock at the door stops my brooding. "If that's Hope, she's an hour early." I limp to the door calling, "*J'arrive.*" I hear Boris's hoarse bark and Jean-Louis's smoker's cough. When I open the door, I see both their noses are upturned, sniffing the air.

"Is something burning in your kitchen?" Jean-Louis asks.

"The potatoes! I forgot them," I screech and bump into Boris as I do an about-face toward the kitchen.

"Permit me to handle it," Jean-Louis says, sweeping by me. In the kitchen, he shrieks, "*Quelle catastrophe!*" A pan clangs onto the tile floor and crisp, blackened potatoes roll into the hall.

Jean-Louis and I, giggling like children, are picking up the hot potatoes and tossing them in the pan, when Hope steps through the open door. Me, in a long white waiter's apron. I slowly unbend and look up at Hope. "Oh-oh, now she knows I'm a lousy cook," I whisper to the scorched odor in the air.

Handing me a bouquet of violets wrapped in cellophane and tied with a purple ribbon, Hope leans over and kisses my forehead. I feel something inside me change, like she's kissed my soul. I realize I've been aching with loneliness, feeling unwanted. And now here she is with flowers.

"Let me do that," she says and gracefully stoops, wrinkling her long, beige linen sheath dress, to pick up the rest of the potatoes scattered about the floor. "They're charcoal broiled," she says kindly and puts them in the pan. Standing behind me, Jean-Louis says, "*Si gentille, si vivante, si charmante.*"

"Meet my niece, Hope Grayson. Hope, this is Jean-Louis Duval. I mentioned him the other day."

He unfurls a handkerchief and wipes his hands, before shaking Hope's hand. "I am your aunt's manager, but I do not manage her kitchen."

"This kitchen needs a manager. The potatoes are burned, and the rooster's not in the pot yet," I whine.

"We will go out to dinner—to Haynes Restaurant," Jean-Louis says.

"Good idea," I agree, "but let's have an *apéritif* first."

Hope, Jean-Louis, and Boris follow me into the living room. Pointing to the sofa, "Have a seat," I say to Hope. Instead she steps across the room to study the wall of photographs. She moves from one frame to the next, from time to time uttering, "Wow!" Jean-Louis and I exchange nods, and follow Hope's walk through scenes from my career. Thinking of Stanley's photos, I whisper to Jean-Louis, "I'm glad my pictures are hanging," as Hope discharges another "Wow."

"You like the photographs?" Jean-Louis asks.

"They're awesome. You were awesome, Aunt Violet."

"Drop the 'aunt.' Just Violet, OK?"

"I'll try. You look fabulous in these pictures. It's exciting to see scenes from your life. Will you tell me about each one, where it was taken, what was going on?"

"Each one? That'll take all night."

"Tell her about them. I will get drinks," Jean-Louis says.

"This one is charming," Hope says, pointing to a photo of me in a sarong and wide-brimmed straw hat.

"It was taken when I was in the Paris production of South Pacific. They'd hired me as an understudy for several parts. The actress playing Lait, the Polynesian girl, broke an ankle in rehearsal, so I got the role for the entire run. That's how it goes. You take whatever they offer and find a way to show what you can do."

"What did you do after South Pacific?"

"When it closed? I got weekend gigs in clubs, but nothing steady for a long time. If you have club work on weekends, on weekdays you're doing other work—like waitressing. And you keep auditioning, going from place to place, showing your stuff." I move to the sofa and sit. Leo, disturbed by the motion, darts from his hiding place under the sofa into the kitchen.

"Between each picture on that wall were weeks of living an ordinary working life in everyday clothes, waiting for a lucky break," I tell her.

"Or for a lucky manager," says Jean-Louis who is bringing a Coke Light and two glasses of ruby-colored kir on a tray. "A lucky, entrepreneurial manager is what one needs," he says handing Hope a kir. The Coke is for me. He lifts his glass in a trembling hand. I'm nervous about his toast, hoping he won't overstate what he or I can offer. He looks like he's trying out for the role of manager, as he straightens the stoop of his narrow shoulders under his black T-shirt and tan linen jacket. The creased blue jeans and highly polished loafers are essential to the costume of a successful manager, but I know the man in this outfit. Good luck has eluded him for ten years or more. His bad luck and mine started at the same time. He learned he's HIV-positive the same week I was diagnosed as diabetic. Good luck now is to be alive, have a pension, good doctors, a roof over one's head, reliable friends, and the company of pets.

"*Santé*," he says, his quivering glass held high. We reply, "*Santé!*" Hope takes in the room as she drinks. With admiring glances at the furniture, the plants, the gallery of photos, she says, "This place looks like a stage set for a play about an artist."

I chuckle and look at Jean-Louis, who says coolly, "This is how an artist should live."

"I'd like to know where and how Paris artists live," Hope says, as if talking to herself.

Jean-Louis says, "You must make the acquaintance of dancers, actors, painters, writers. You must meet chic, young people. I will take you to clubs in the Marais and the Oberkampf district. You must promenade with me on the Champs-Elysées. I'll take you backstage at Le Lido and introduce you."

"You must go to the Moulin Rouge. It's just up the street on Clichy. I'm sure you saw it. Years ago, I could have introduced you to the crowd there, mostly musicians. But my circle, like the song says, has dwindled down to a precious few," I say as I get to my feet. "Keep Hope entertained. I'm going to freshen my makeup."

In my bedroom at the dressing table, I turn on the new fluorescent bulbs. I take off my apron and lean toward the mirror. Tinted, frizzy hair; thinning eyebrows penciled kohl; pouches under the eyes; puffy cheeks spotted with freckles and little, black moles; wrinkles around my mouth. Rouging my cheeks, layering on a red lipstick, and brushing my hair away from my face improve me slightly. I wish I had something to wear other than this five-year-old beige pantsuit. It's good enough for Haynes; after all, it's not La Tour d'Argent.

Suddenly I see a burst of light, like a camera's flash, near the altar of images of Josephine. A life-sized Josephine in top hat, white tie, and tails, appears in the light. She says "Wouldn't it be wonderful to make her the next beautiful black music hall star? *Bonne chance!*" then disappears. I get a whiff of bananas. Breathing hard, I let out a gasp.

"I heard something. What is it?" calls Hope.

"It's Josephine!" I squeal.

"Ah, another vision. Your aunt imagines Josephine Baker visits her from time to time."

"I heard that, Jean-Louis. I'm not imagining. She was just here." Standing before the altar, I lift a framed portrait of Josephine from the corner table, kiss the picture, and say, "I'm going to introduce you to Hope someday."

"Come, Violetta. Let's go to dinner," Jean-Louis coaxes from the living room. Hope and Jean-Louis are waiting with worried faces.

"It's not like I've seen a ghost. It was only Josephine," I say calmly, and bend toward my cane on the floor beside the sofa. Hope picks it up and hands it to me. Jean-Louis, with Boris close behind, starts toward the door.

"The walk to Haynes will clear your head," he says to me. Behind his glasses, he winks at Hope. I see conspiracy in his wink.

"Someday I'll introduce you to my Josephine Baker," I tell Hope.

On the landing outside the apartment, I lock the door, turn around, feel for the railing, and start downstairs. I am steadied by Hope who holds my arm.

10

What used to be a ten-minute walk to Haynes Restaurant on rue Clauzel has become a half-hour hike at my pace and with Jean-Louis's shaky gait. On entering the restaurant, Benny Luke greets us with warm familiarity. Luke's a retired dancer. His every movement appears choreographed. He kisses our hands, Hope's and mine, embraces Jean-Louis, and bows toward Boris. Unfurling his arm in a *porte-a-bras*, he says, "Your table is waiting for you." Then he steps behind the bar, polishes glasses, and sways to Ellington's "Mood Indigo."

The restaurant is small and intimate. On the walls are framed photos of celebrity expatriates living in France and the rich and famous who've dined here when they passed through Paris. "You may not think so tonight, because so few folks are here," I tell Hope, "but for half a century this place has been a Mecca for black Americans, especially jazz musicians, painters, and writers. It's still a crossroads for some blacks—tourists and residents. There was a time when you had to come here to find out what's happening."

The aroma of soul food—fried chicken, roast pork, collard greens—takes me back to Louisville church suppers and Sunday dinners in Harlem homes. A "nostalgia restaurant" is what Stanley called Haynes. I can almost hear voices of Negroes playing the dozens, laughing, and some woman singing the blues with a dude on guitar. When I come to Haynes I'm reminded of what I miss about the States.

When the waiter comes, Jean-Louis and I order southern fried chicken, greens, rice, and red beans. Hope will have spare ribs with a salad. While waiting, Jean-Louis and I eat an entire basket of cornbread.

"It's like a gallery. Walk around and look at the pictures," Jean-Louis tells her.

She gets up and goes over to the wall. I watch her, knowing she'll come across the photo of Stanley and me, his trumpet on one arm and his other arm around my waist. When she sees it, Hope returns to our table and says, "There's a cool picture of you with Uncle Stanley over there!"

"It was taken at the Mars Club on the Right Bank in '67."

"He's looking at you with adoring eyes. You must miss his music."

"I miss him. And I miss his music and his musician friends." I want to tell her about my monologues with his pictures, but I'm afraid she wouldn't understand.

When we're served, Jean-Louis and I focus on our plates, with no effort at conversation. Hope, only sampling the food, looks on as if our appetites embarrass her. I'm thinking: she's definitely Marie's daughter.

"Tasty ribs," I tell her. "Pick them up. Eat with your fingers."

She smiles and looks about at the other table of diners. Jean-Louis remarks, "Only tourists are here tonight. It is their August occupation of Paris. Hope, I wish you could see the regular crowd."

After dinner, Jean-Louis says he has a rendezvous at a new club. He invites Hope to join him. Instead, she offers to take me home. She and I come back to rue Frochot by taxi.

The café is open, so I suggest we stop in for coffee. André is at work behind the bar. Other than the habitués at the bar, the café is empty. They turn briefly from the television game show to mumble, "*Bonsoir, mesdames.*" Hope and I are drawn to the table where we first met. André comes over; we shake hands. He nods toward Hope, who flashes a smile at him. We order coffee.

While we wait, I ask the question that has been on my mind all evening: "Have you written to Marie, told her you've seen me?"

"I phoned. And, yes, I told her."

"What'd she say?"

"She asked how you are, wanted to know how you look. I told her that she and you ought to be in touch. She asked for your address and phone number."

"What else did she say?"

"She asked about my plans."

"Uh-huh, as any mom would. What did you tell her?"

"I told her I'm making plans. Then she had a lot to say about show business being risky, budgeting my money, being careful about men—the usual advice."

"Gives a lot of advice, does she?"

"Yes, and it's useful—most of the time." I can tell Hope doesn't want to say much about her relations with Marie.

André brings us coffee and returns to the bar. I take a sip of coffee before saying, "Marie and I never had the chance to become close to each other."

"I think she's sorry about that. But maybe I can help bring you close."

"I don't know if you can make things better between us. But you can learn from our mistaken ways and patch up your relationship with your sister," I tell her. She looks surprised, like she's wondering how I figured out she and Faith aren't on the best of terms.

"I've gathered you and Faith aren't as close as you should be. You as much as said so."

"We've got different interests, different lifestyles. We really don't have much in common," Hope says.

"What's happened between you two?"

"Nothing happened. She takes exception to my way of life, and I've got reservations about hers. Isn't that what happened between you and Mom?"

"I could have been more honest about my situation. I didn't have to make Marie feel I was on top of the world and she was on the bottom. And she shouldn't have made me feel I was in a trashy business. It wasn't sisterly." I'm getting stirred up. The doctor's told me to try to be calm. I sip the coffee, and that doesn't calm me; it only makes my heart beat faster.

"I've got friends in Atlanta who are more like sisters to me than Faith is."

"I'm sure you do. Girlfriends who are sister substitutes. They take the place and time in your life that Faith should occupy." I'm growing agitated and preachy. From the blank stare she's giving me, I know it's a sermon Hope doesn't want to hear.

"OK, OK," she says with a crafty squint of her eyes. "If you make some space in your life for your sister, I'll make space in my life for mine. A deal?" She holds up an open palm, and reflexively I slap her a high five.

"*D'accord.* It's a deal," I say. For a moment, I'm stunned. Before I know how I feel about contacting Marie, I've made a pact with her daughter. Making the deal somehow clears the air. Hope now looks as peaceful as a bunny rabbit. Relaxing a little, we slip into casual café talk. She tells me about a film she saw last week. We review dinner at Haynes, agree that the food, improved with herbs and sauces, may be even better than soul food in the States. Then she wants to know if I ever "long for Louisville."

"Long for Louisville? No, but I regret not spending more time there with Hampton. If I had what they call a kindred spirit in the family, it was Hampton."

"I've always wondered what was he like."

"He was a dreamer. When he was young, he had names for the horses he hoped to own. Named them for comic book characters: Captain Marvel and Superman's Surprise. Hampton and Papa were at the kitchen table early one winter morning. It was a school day. I'd made cheese grits for breakfast and was packing our lunches. Hampton began telling Papa about dreaming of owning a horse farm, what he'd name his horses, how he'd place them in races. Papa tapped his bowl with a spoon. Quietly but firmly, Papa said, 'Have you forgotten yourself, boy? Forgotten you're a Negro? Don't you know you can never be a major player in the racing game? Get a good education. Be a doctor or a lawyer, something that's a service to our people.'

"That day Hampton and I played hooky from school. We went to the track but avoided the stables where Papa worked. Hampton was moping, and I moped with him. Sitting for a long time on the top row in the stands, he asked me if Papa was right. I told him, 'No, Papa's got no crystal ball. He can't see what you and I are going to do.'

"He leaned into me. 'Damn right, he can't know what I'm going to do,' he said. I hugged Hampton, who didn't pull away like boys that age usually did.

After that, though, he acted discouraged. He started talking like Papa.

"But you asked if I miss Louisville. I was sixteen when I left Louisville. When I've visited since, it wasn't at all the way it was in my day. Integration changed things. Black and white kids go to the same schools. The races intermingle, but I'm not comfortable mixing with whites there. I don't trust white Louisville." I pause for a while to see if she understands me. Hope nods slowly, so I go on. "When I came along, there was colored Louisville and white Louisville. Schools were segregated. Colored folks weren't allowed in public parks and swimming pools, weren't even allowed in the public library. Movie houses were separate and definitely not equal. We got films weeks after they were shown in the white theaters. And downtown, Jim Crow ruled.

"I'd seen a dress in the window of Stewart's. I went downtown and walked by the store window nearly every day just to see it. Then one day it disappeared from the window. I'd saved enough money, I figured, to buy that dress for Easter. I was old enough—almost fifteen—to buy my own clothes. So I went in, found the dress, and said to a saleslady—white, of course, 'I'd like to see that dress.'

"She said, 'You can look at it, but you can't try it on. Store policy.'

"Of course, I knew what she meant, but I wanted to push the matter. 'Why can't I?'

"'Because you're a nigger. Niggers can't try on clothes in this store. You can buy it, but if it don't fit, too bad. No exchanging. It's store policy.'

"I got out of that store in a hurry. I was angry, so angry I cried all the way home." Remembering that day still upsets me. With a sip of coffee I swallow the lump in my throat.

Hope says, "Those were tough times. That must have been very painful."

"It was painful. It would take all night to tell you about all the hurtful, humiliating experiences I had in Louisville on account of race. So do I long for Louisville? Hell, no. Now, Paris, if I'm away for only a weekend, I long for Paris. Not just this neighborhood where I always feel at home. I feel good about myself anywhere in Paris. When I arrived in Paris in '52, I felt entitled to anything and everything that was public—parks, cinemas, nightclubs, cafés, restaurants, buses, the Métro—whatever. I didn't know how browbeaten and stressed I'd felt in Louisville, and even in New York City. Didn't know I'd felt oppressed, if that's the right word, until I came to Paris. Paris let me find myself and be proud to be who I am. When I'm away from Paris, that's a feeling that I miss. Louisville never let me feel good about who I was."

"Aside from Louisville, is there anything about America that you miss?"

"I miss my folks. Not family particularly, but black folks, African Americans. I miss the hum of our talk, down-home slang, deep laughter, ways of signifying. I miss our spin on racial matters, politicians, the police, and celebrities. Comments at the hairdresser on stories in *Jet* and *Ebony*. I miss soul food—our cuisine—especially at celebrations that call for feasting: weddings and funerals, Thanksgiving and Christmas. And I miss our music, especially church music that makes you clap hands and say 'Amen.' Blues so mournful you want to weep. Jazz that makes you tap your feet, rock your shoulders to the beat."

Hope nods, "That's for sure." With a flick of her wrist, she lets André know we want more coffee. Then she says, "How'd you hook up with Jean-Louis?"

"I'd noticed him at cabarets and jazz clubs, scouting talent, watching audiences respond to acts. Always the natty dresser, in any crowd Jean-Louis was easy to spot. If he didn't like an act, he left in a flash. He came to L'Abbaye, Gordon Heath's nightclub that was in Saint-Germain-des-Pres one night when I was singing. Stayed for the entire set. He told me he liked my voice and wanted to represent me. From the get-go, Jean-Louis treated me like an important artist, a grand talent. He was good for me professionally. Now he's a very good friend."

I turn the conversation back to her, to get an idea of what she sees in her future. "What do you want to be doing fifteen years from now?"

"At thirty-nine? I'd like to be established in musical theater and television, probably in New York or Los Angeles. Getting started here, I think, might be an advantage. Being able to say 'I worked in Paris,' should have a certain cachet in New York."

"What about marriage and kids?" I ask. The older I get, the more I regret not having the son we had to share memories of his daddy's life and mine. I can't talk to her about little Stanley, not here. Within three months he was born and had died. Born with lungs too little to support him. The morning we went to the hospital expecting to bring him home, we were told he'd just died. Laid out in a tiny casket—all in blue my boy was buried. At the cemetery, Stanley played a variation on "Taps" for little Stanley, not the way they bugle "Taps" at a military funeral, but mournfully and sweetly like a lullaby. I cried and saw Stanley crying while he sounded his lament for his son. For weeks afterward, at home I stood over the empty bassinet weeping. Finding me there, Stanley would take out his trumpet and blow his blues "Taps." The three of us—little Stanley, Stanley, and me—we would have made a fine family.

Hope is silent for a while. She's sensed the gloom that invaded me. Finally, she says, "I'd like to have a family, a good marriage, and two or three kids. But I want to build my career first." She lifts her chin on saying "career."

At that moment, André comes to our table. "You're out late tonight, Madame Violet. It's one o'clock, closing time." Noticing the drift of other customers toward the door, I reach for my purse.

"Coffee is on the house. I've closed the books, done the accounting for the night," he yawns. Turning to Hope, he asks, "Do you live in this arrondissement?"

"I'm staying in the fifth, near Luxembourg," she says flatly.

"I'm going in that direction. I'll take you. I've got a motor scooter and an extra helmet. I need ten minutes to stack chairs and lock up. Take Madame Violet home. I'll wait here for you."

"OK," Hope says.

I'd thought about fixing them up, but they don't need my matchmaking. It's all arranged. No overtures necessary. Hope helps me to my feet and toward the door. Outside the café, I take in the cool night air and notice who is cruising and being cruised. Nightclub lights are flashing. It's desperation time. Men drive to the corner and beckon prostitutes, who lean wigged heads and brazen breasts into car windows to negotiate what fifty euros will buy. On the sidewalk, tourists, voyeurs, and sexual adventurers jostle each other.

I'm glad André's offered Hope a ride. I don't want her propositioned in my neighborhood.

With an arm around my shoulders, Hope moves me across the street and helps me up the stairs at a pretty fast pace. I don't know whether she's just eager to have a ride or she's come to her senses and sees that André is a good catch. I'm cool. I don't say a word about him.

"You can sleep on my sofa if you want to," I offer.

"Not tonight, thanks. I've got to walk the dogs. But some other time." She takes the key, unlocks my door, and ushers me inside. With kisses on my cheeks, she turns to leave. Before closing the door, Hope says, "I'll phone you tomorrow."

In a hurry to get a glimpse of them from the window, I stumble in the dark, almost fall over Leo, and topple the little table beneath the mirror.

"Damn those decorators! That table wasn't there before." I miss crashing into the mirror by inches. I turn on the light, step around the table, and hobble across the living room and into my bedroom. Opening the window, I see André astride the scooter's twin seat. In her sheath dress, helmeted Hope sits sidesaddle and loops her arms around his waist. The motor sputters and they drive off. I blow them a kiss, wishing them love. If only Stanley could be here to see them—and to hold me, kiss me, and make me feel young again.

11

The early morning tint of an orange sky spills into my bedroom. I'm lying on my left side facing the Josephine altar. I focus on the photo of her in her World War II Free French Air Force uniform. When I think of her ambition and courage, I feel like a coward, afraid to face an ordinary day.

I stretch my legs and hear bones creak. Bend the knees several times before getting up, the physical therapist told me. My right knee is swollen again, arthritis for sure. Roll over to the edge of the bed; sit up, feet firmly planted on the floor, then float up. "Float up," the therapist said. Ha! Battle gravity and struggle to get up. Well, here goes. Ugh, just getting up is tiring.

It's *jeudi*, Thursday, or is it Friday? The nurse is coming today, so it must be *vendredi*—Friday. "Another day, another chance," Stanley said every morning. Another chance for the vampire-nurse's weekly visit for a blood sample, for chitchat with Jean-Louis, and for me to buy the lucky Euromillions ticket. What has my life come to? I used to jump out of bed, turn on some dance music, shimmy and shake to the rhythm, warming up for the day's work. Now when I hear dance music, it just reminds me of routines these feet can't do anymore.

Get up, feed Leo and change his water, have a bite to eat, bathe a little, get dressed, and wait. Wait for somebody to come, for something to happen. Hope said she'd call. I want to hear about what she and André did, not that she'll tell me. After all, it's none of my business. But it would be good if they got together. About the same age, intelligent, same kind of good looks. They could be brother and sister. But that could work against them.

Young people today seem to be attracted to opposites. The popular black models are always photographed with their blond boyfriends; black star athletes hook up with white girls. There's a fascination now with different looks, different backgrounds. Josephine crossed over, too. Maybe it's always been that way for some people. Stanley had his Swedish fling before he found he could be content with his own kind. And Hope's sister, Faith, married to a Jewish guy. Marie may like him now, but I bet she had to get some prejudices out of her system before she learned to like him.

Maybe that's how to approach Marie. Write to her about how times have changed. Ask her to send news about the family and Louisville. I suppose she could take it the wrong way and think I'm meddling. But I ought to send some kind of letter to Marie to start working on my deal with Hope.

Dear Marie,

Hope and I have met again. She's a fine young woman. She told me about your marriage to Billy Knox and about Faith's wedding. I'm happy for you. I'd like to be in touch with you and Faith. I don't write many letters, but if we send notes from time to time, perhaps we can get a fresh start.

Your sister,
Violet

Writing this little letter took almost two hours. Several crumpled sheets of paper—false starts—in the wastebasket. I'm looking for an envelope, even though I don't have Marie's address, when Jean-Louis knocks. I go to the door. He and Boris prance in. Jean-Louis is breathless. His face is flushed.

"Hey, you look like you got lucky last night," I tell him.

"Violetta, we got lucky last night. I met Christophe Michelet, the new manager of the Métropole. He is ecstatic about the Christmas program I proposed! I told him you have a mother-and-daughter act. Presenting Violet and Hope Fields, *Les Jingle Belles*. Pop Christmas music, a few French religious carols, and Negro spirituals. Singing duets and a little dancing. Hope can do the dance numbers. Christophe adores the idea."

"She's not my daughter."

"She looks enough like you to be your daughter."

"She may not like the idea."

"She will do anything to see you onstage again, and she will adore working with you. It is the chance of a lifetime for Hope—and for you. I'm taking you out to *déjeuner*. One must celebrate and make plans."

"A restaurant where I can wear this T-shirt and slacks?"

"Yes, the bistro at the corner. *Allons-y.*"

I haven't seen Jean-Louis so excited in years. He's acting like his younger self. His mood is contagious. I feel a little pep in my step as I follow him downstairs and to the street. The bistro has a lively clientele that comes as much for show-biz contacts as for the food. Mirrored walls, crisp, white tablecloths, flowers on each table, it's rather pretty. I get a whiff of the grilled salmon and steamed potatoes served at the next table, and suddenly I'm hungry. Jean-Louis and I order the same thing: *pâté de foie de canard* and *lapin dijonnais*. He chooses a bottle of Brouilly, and I don't refuse when the waiter pours.

It's like old times, talking business over lunch. Jean-Louis is speaking louder than usual, not only so that I can hear him, but also so others will know we're in the business again. When our waiter brings the *pâté*, Jean-Louis closes the little notebook with graph paper on which he's scribbled promotional slogans, costume ideas, and lighting directions. I hum a few Christmas tunes between bites, and tell him the titles. We try to recall names of producers, dance coaches, and set designers. He suggests a time table and lists things to be done. After lunch and several cups of coffee, we're still talking. Only then something tells me that I should ask, "When can we expect a contract with the Métropole?"

"Ah, who can say?" He shrugs. His eyes avoid mine. And I know this *déjeuner* has been a rehearsal for a meeting he hopes to have. I know, too, that Christophe Michelet is probably an assistant manager with no clout. Anyway, it's nice to be taken out to lunch.

A rush of reality slows Jean-Louis's pace and mine as he and Boris accompany me to rue Frochot. "*Non, merci,*" I say when he offers to help me up the stairs. "Instead, walk over to the Métropole and speak with Monsieur Michelet and his boss about a contract." Jean-Louis knows I'm annoyed with him and myself for dreaming about a show that may not happen. It's not the first time.

I return to the reality of the rest of my day: watching TV and waiting for the vampire nurse. *C'est la vie.* The nurse's visit to draw a little blood and review my medications leaves me exhausted. I take a nap and wake up after midnight to the buzz of the TV set. While I'm undressing, Josephine appears. She's only partially dressed or undressed. Ropes of pearls crisscross her body; her breasts are bare.

She looks young and flirtatious. She hums a tune I don't get at first. Then she sings it: "There's No Business Like Show Business." Josephine smiles as she ends the song. She says, "Violet, you can do it. You've still got a great voice."

"Sure, I can still sing, but I can't dance, can't move like I used to."

"You can still dazzle the crowd. It's your chance for a reprise—a comeback."

I want her to stay a while. But she turns away and disappears, leaving her fragrance behind.

12

At the American Hospital in the waiting room of Dr. Chang's office, I pick up a copy of *France Soir*. It's yesterday's paper: 1 *septembre*, St. Gilles' feast day. The front-page headline is *Rentrée à Paris*, with the number of autoroute accidents that occurred during the end-of-vacation rush back to Paris. I scan the entertainment pages, then turn to the horoscope. Born under Gemini, one is advised to stay close to home and welcome houseguests. I've been at home, ready to welcome Hope and take her in. I thought I'd hear from her, since she had to move yesterday. Maybe she's staying on at rue Gay-Lussac. Or maybe she's moved to a youth hostel, and would rather be with smelly strangers and their backpacks than sleep at my place. At first I felt she'd be a burden. But now I want her to come and live with me for a while. She could help me with errands and chores. Besides, I'm lonely and sometimes scared of being alone.

Dr. Chang's nurse, a slim, perky woman, opens the office door and calls my name. She escorts me to the examining room, tells me to undress, and hands me a hospital gown to cover myself. I'm lying down on the examining table when Dr. Chang comes in. His questions and inquiring fingers make me think of changes in my body. I used to be vain about my looks. When I got dolled up, I was a knockout. I had a good figure, smooth brown skin, full head of hair, great legs, and a groovy, hip-swinging walk. The years have taken their toll. Nobody will want to see this body onstage. Jean-Louis is marketing me with photographs taken twenty years ago. The pictures lie. No matter. No one will fall for the package he's hawking. Still I want to get in shape just in case, by some miracle, he does somehow manage to book a show.

Tapping my knees with a rubber hammer, Chang looks up, frowns over his horn-rimmed glasses, and taps again. He feels my ankles and legs and says nothing, He's serious, thorough, young, Hong Kong-born and American-trained—a Johns Hopkins diploma on the wall.

"Well, Doc, you think these feet will ever dance again?"

"If you walk more, twenty minutes every day, your feet will know what they're supposed to do. You're going to need some tests. I'm recommending a stricter diet and an exercise program." He turns to his desk and makes notes on a form.

"I'll be getting more exercise," I say with fantasies about a rehearsal routine. He ignores my remark. Handing me three prescriptions, he says, "If there are no changes over the next three months, I'd like to hospitalize you for some procedures."

"What procedures?" The last time he saw me, he said if the circulation in my leg fails completely, they might need to amputate. I'm wondering if that's what he's calling "procedures."

"It's too soon to tell precisely what may be needed. It all depends on how you respond to a new medication and how you manage your regime."

"I don't want my leg..." I can't even say it.

"Amputation would be a measure of last resort, Madame Fields. If everything works, we won't ever need to do it."

"Everything better work, Doc." I want him to promise, but doctors don't make promises. Chang isn't likely to give me odds; he doesn't look like a betting man. I put the prescriptions in my purse and reach out for his handshake. I squeeze his hand, to communicate my anxiety about my condition.

Leaning heavily on my cane, I take the elevator to the lobby where Monique is seated. She's rocking gently to the music piped through her earbuds. Removing them, she gets up and smiles at me with an optimistic, *"Tout va bien?"* I review what happened. Finally, I say, *"Oui."*

Monique, holding my elbow, guides me on the walk through the hospital garden to her car in the parking lot. The midday traffic is hectic. At midday, Parisians on the way to lunch drive as if late to the Last Supper. Clutching the steering wheel, Monique constantly changes lanes. Her driving makes me nervous. I should've taken a taxi instead. Rain splatters the windshield. We're now in stop-and-start traffic, with horns blaring and brakes shrieking. I close my eyes and see in the print of the International Herald Tribune: "Parisian Dancer and Elderly Expatriate Killed in Traffic Accident." At last Monique says, "Rue Frochot, your street. You can open your eyes now."

Monique pulls up at the entrance of my building. She gets out and comes around to help me out of the car. Across the street, Hope is standing outside the café. She has two suitcases and a backpack. I wave and call to her, "Hello, Hope." Can it be that she's come to stay with me?

"That's my niece. Give her a hand with her suitcases." Holding open the door of my building, I wait while Monique crosses the street and talks to Hope. Leaving Monique with her baggage, Hope comes over to me with me her big smile and three kisses. She says, "I'm waiting for André to take me to his mother's place. She wants somebody to take care of her apartment and forward her mail, that sort of thing, while she's in Africa."

"So you're moving into his mother's place. Well, what's it like?" I want to know if it's much better than mine.

"I haven't seen it, but I'm sure it's very nice. It's in Neuilly near the hospital where she works. She's a psychiatrist. She works with AIDS patients, their partners and families."

André drives up in a BMW. In a rush, Hope says she'll see me soon and dashes to relieve Monique of the suitcases. André waves and calls out, "*A bientôt*, Madame Violet."

I turn away feeling he's betrayed me. He'd said it was good for me to have her here. Then he lures her away, sets her up in his mother's damn place. I'm not speaking to that—that son-of-a-psychiatrist.

Monique offers to walk upstairs with me, but I send her on her way. I want to be alone. One step at a time, I climb up the three flights and unlock the door. Opening it, I look down to find faithful Leo at the door purring his affection. I collapse on the sofa. Leo crawls onto my lap. Out loud, I tell myself, "What can you expect? You introduced him to Hope, and he made off with her."

I feel a trickle of tears, dab my eyes, clear my throat, and phone Jean-Louis. He knows at once that something is wrong, but he's taking Boris to the vet and doesn't have time talk now. Too busy to talk to an old friend?

I drift from room to room. This place looks strange, looks like it belongs to somebody else. And to think I wanted it fixed up so that she would like it and want to spend time here. I try not to feel sorry for myself, but I can't help it. Curling up on the sofa, I cry myself to sleep.

-A knock at the door wakes me up. Pushing aside the sofa pillow damp with tears, I get to my feet, walk to the door, and open it to find Jean-Louis standing there.

"Violetta, you have been crying. What has happened?" Jean-Louis comes in. I hold open the door, expecting Boris behind him.

"Where's Boris?"

"*Au vétérinaire.* Prostate surgery on the old boy. It should go well. But I need coffee." He lifts his chin and tries to look brave.

Walking behind Jean-Louis to the kitchen, I blurt out, "Hope's moving into André's mother's apartment, and I'm pissed."

"*Ooo-la-la!* Hope and André are together. But you wanted that, *n'est-ce pas?*"

"Yes, but I wanted her to spend some time with me. Now I won't see her. You got this place all fixed up for nothing."

While filling the coffee maker, he says, "You imagine things. You imagined she would live with you. You did not invite her to live here, did you?"

"No, but I thought she'd want to live here."

"Some people need to be invited. And what about you and her mother? Before Hope can trust you completely, you should make peace with the mother."

"I wrote a letter to Marie, but I haven't mailed it yet."

"Send the letter to your sister. You need to unite your family. I believe that is why Hope is here. She wants family." He pauses to light a cigarette. "I had a rendezvous today with Christophe and others at the Métropole. They want to book the show. They want you and Hope to audition next week. So you must begin rehearsals with her immediately."

"Jean-Louis, is this for real?"

"Yes, it is real. After the audition, we get the contract for dates in mid-December. You told me to go for a contract. I did. I took your CDs and video and a proposal to Christophe. He and his associates adore your work and the idea for the show."

I heave a big sigh. Moments later I'm in a cold sweat. "I need a cigarette. We've got to do some planning."

"Violetta, we did the plan last week over lunch, remember? I put all we talked about in the proposal. Now you and Hope must work on an act. It must look polished, like you have been doing it for years."

I'm lighting a cigarette with one hand and feeling my hair with the other. "I've got to see a hairdresser. And I'm going to need a chic outfit for this audition."

"You need a total makeover. I will arrange that."

"What about Hope?"

"She looks perfect—just as she is."

"When do we tell her?"

"I will call her and ask her to meet us here tonight around ten. It's her grand chance. I must go now to visit Boris."

My heart is pumping fast. It's a terrific opportunity for Hope and me. And for Jean-Louis. It's good for his morale. And mine.

13

It's early evening, and I'm like a spinning top wound tight with excitement. Release the cord and I'll reel out of control. At the medicine cabinet, I take a tranquilizer, and then lie on the sofa to calm myself. But my heart and mind are still racing. I can see posters plastered all over Paris: "Violet Fields appearing with her daughter Hope Fields." If Hope Grayson could become Greta Grayson, she most certainly can use the name Hope Fields. But being assigned a new mother, if only for the stage, may be a problem. What if the act catches on, we get some press, and are outed? I can see the headlines: "False mother/Fake daughter." What if Marie takes offense? What if I don't relate to Hope like a mother and it ruins the show? And what do I tell people when word is out? They'll say, "I never knew you had a daughter. Who was the father? Stanley?" What if Hope rejects the idea altogether, says she doesn't want a fictitious relationship? Better present it to Hope gently, and afterward check to find out how Marie feels about it.

I'll send my letter to Marie. Follow up with a phone call. Tell Marie about the act and ask, "May I borrow your daughter?" Maybe she won't mind at all, what with her favoring the Knox kids over her own, like Hope said.

If we're a big hit—Hope and me—we could take our act on the road. Maybe play London and New York, our names in lights on Broadway. The notion of playing on Broadway pulls me out of a fantasy state and into real-world action. I better make coffee and get out of these old jeans and into something else. The blue Moroccan caftan makes me feel regal. I get up and go into the bedroom to search through the armoire for the caftan. Just as I find it, I think I hear Josephine singing. It's her voice from a distance—perhaps from a radio in the apartment above mine. Her voice comes closer. Standing in the bedroom window, Josephine is in her top hat, white tie, and tails. She's singing "White Christmas." I don't recall ever having heard her sing it. "May your days be merry and bright / And may all your Christmases be white." As she croons the lyrics, I walk toward her.

"You and the girl will be sensational," she says, "Lift her on high, let her soar. She has the gift. I'll be with you, watching over you." She slips through the window and is gone. At the window, I look down at the street and see the usual evening scene. I don't see anybody in top hat and tails. As I put on the caftan, it occurs to me that I better tell Hope about Josephine soon. After all, she may be onstage with us.

A few minutes after ten, there's a knock at the door. I call out, "*J'arrive.*" Lifting the caftan so as not to trip, I hobble to the door. Jean-Louis, looking glum, stands in the doorway. On the right sleeve of his jacket is a black armband. My first thought is that one of his sisters has died. He'll have to go to the funeral. Plans for the Métropole will collapse.

"Who died, Jean-Louis?" I ask softly.

"*Boris est mort. Une crise cardiaque.*" He chokes up.

"During the operation?"

"No, after. The operation went well, but his heart was stressed by it." He steps toward me and I hug him. Holding him in an awkward pose, my arms around his hips, I look beyond him where Hope is staring at us.

"Have I come too early?" she asks.

"No, right on time. Jean-Louis has had a tragedy. Boris died," I explain as I release my hold on him.

"I'm very sorry. Should we postpone the meeting?" She seems eager to leave.

Recovering instantly, Jean-Louis says, "No, we must meet now. We have urgent business to discuss." He removes his glasses and, with a black silk handkerchief, wipes his eyes. The armband, the handkerchief—I wonder if he's had them on hand thinking he'd be wearing them for me.

"Come in, sit down, and have some coffee. I'll make a pot."

Jean-Louis nods and totters to the sofa. Hope says, "Let me make the coffee. You both take it black, don't you?"

"Yes, black," I answer for both of us and join Jean-Louis on the sofa. My old coffee table would be useful now. Instead I have three plastic stools, a knockoff of some Italian design, where the table stood. When Hope returns, we are holding hands. He drops my hand, reaches for a cup, his hand trembling. He tells Hope to take a seat. Jean-Louis is in charge again.

"We have the chance of a lifetime," he says. "The Métropole Music Hall is reopening in November with a big spectacle. It will draw large audiences. The spectacle closes on 6 December. On 14 December our show opens for three days. French and American Christmas music arranged to tell a holiday story. Musical theater, with popular holiday songs, gospel, a few traditional carols, and good choreography."

For the moment, Boris is forgotten. Jean-Louis stands and paces between us, his tail feathers high, commanding attention in the style of a super salesman, selling us on the show. It's the pitch he used at the Métropole, I'm sure. He crows, "Small company—a dozen singers and dancers, girls like Odile and Monique, excellent dancers who also have good voices. And two or three gorgeous boys. The featured singer and star of the program is the celebrated Violet Fields. Performing with her is the new sensation, her daughter, Hope Fields, in *Les Jingle Belles*." He stops pacing in front of Hope, waiting for her reaction.

She's rigid as a statue, upright in the chair, her face fixed in a prim expression. In a pale blue sweatshirt with Spelman College across her chest and blue jeans, she looks more like a serious student than a performer.

Impatient with Hope's silence, Jean-Louis sighs, "*Alors*, what do you think of it?"

"*Les Belles de Noël* would be smoother and easier to understand. And…" She pauses as if thinking about what more she wants to say. "And could you say women instead of girls?" So that's irritated her. "And how can you say I'm a sensational singer? You've never heard me sing."

"What about the mother-daughter stuff?" I ask.

"That's cool with me, if you're comfortable with it," she says matter-of-factly.

"Hey, I love the idea. But will Marie?"

"You need to ask her. It'll make her think about my place in her life—and in yours." She looks into my eyes like she's seeing inside me, seeing the empty space that could hold love for a daughter. It makes me edgy.

I say, "I wrote a letter to Marie, but I don't have her address, so I haven't mailed it."

Hope stands. From a pocket in her jeans, she hands me an envelope addressed to Marie. She gives me a slip of paper and says pointedly, "And this is her phone number."

"OK, I'll mail the letter tomorrow. And I'll call her in a few days—after she gets my letter." I want to ask Hope if she's written to Faith, but this isn't the moment.

Jean-Louis, animated and eager, says to Hope, "I need to hear you sing solo and do some duets with Violetta. We must prepare well for the audition. Are you available to rehearse tomorrow afternoon?" He's asking Hope. He knows I'm free.

"Yes, I have no plans for tomorrow."

"I have reserved a studio with a piano and pianist for the afternoon. It is not far from here." He hands her a card with the address. "You know the place," he says to me. "Remember Claudine Roulin, the Arlésienne pianist? She still plays for rehearsals."

"Who can forget her in her black lace shawl, hair dyed jet black, and skin that looks like chicken feet?" I wish he knew a younger accompanist, somebody Hope could relate to.

"*Alors*, Hope, do you want to do it?"

"I'll give it a try." She breaks open her big smile like a cork popping out of a bottle of champagne. And I know she's on board.

"Tomorrow," he says, "we all will be there at two." Helping me up from the sofa, Jean-Louis says solemnly, "I will come for you after I arrange for the burial."

In the excitement, I'd forgotten Boris. I pat his black armband and give Jean-Louis a sympathetic squeeze. He and Hope are about to leave when I hear humming in the bedroom.

"Did you hear that?" I ask them.

"I heard something," Hope says.

"It's Leo," Jean-Louis says.

Hearing his name, Leo purrs, pads out of the bathroom, and comes to us in the hall. At the door, we have the usual exchange of kisses. Closing the door behind them, I hear Jean-Louis tell Hope, "*Sa vie est dominée par un fantôme.*"

As fast as I can, I go to the bedroom, hoping to see Josephine. Too late. She's been and gone. Her fragrance is still in the air.

***

Jean-Louis and I arrive promptly at the studio, a bare loft except for a grand piano at one end, mirrors at the other end, stone walls, and two ceiling-to-floor windows with a view of rooftops and chimneys. Claudine Roulin, seated at the piano, is playing. Hope, standing behind Claudine, softly sings:

"Il est né, le divin enfant, / jour de fête aujourd'hui sur terre;

Il est né, le divin enfant, / chantons tous son avènement."

"Ahh, she has the voice of an angel," Jean-Louis whispers.

"When she was a kid, she had it in her. I told you she's good."

"A true bel canto. She's perfect," he says, clapping vigorously as he strides toward Hope. "If you can dance as beautifully as you sing, our success is certain."

Claudine and I greet each other and shake hands. Jean-Louis kisses her sallow cheeks. From the breast pocket of his jacket, he takes out a card with a list of numbers he wants her to play.

Hope's voice is stronger and more lyrical than I'd expected. Her mezzo-soprano and my alto-contralto are in perfect harmony. We know the words of the same songs, most of them anyway. We do solos for a few bars then join in duets. It's as if we've sung

104

together before. Claudine knows the music or improvises on our songs: "Jingle Bells," "Winter Wonderland," "White Christmas," a rock and roll "Go Tell It on the Mountain," then solemnly "Silent Night" and "Ave Maria." Jean-Louis is obviously pleased with our renditions, exclaiming between numbers, "Superb! *Sensationnel!*"

"We've got to end with something lively," I propose. "Let's try 'Joy to the World.'" I hum the tune for Claudine, who quickly catches on and gives it a gospel swing. Singing together, hands clapping, "Joy to the World" lifts Hope into the air. She spins and leaps around the studio with graceful steps, like a well trained ballerina. In a trance, she continues to dance and Claudine plays until Hope winds down and lowers her torso, bends her knees with one foot forward in a curtain call curtsy. Jean-Louis and I applaud wildly.

"Formidable! We will end the program with that 'Joy' number and the dance. One more rehearsal and we're ready to audition," Jean-Louis says, dizzy with excitement. After the session, he leaves for the Métropole to schedule the audition.

I'm tired out by the rehearsal, but it's time for a talk with Hope. So I ask her to taxi home with me and come up to my apartment.

In the living room, Hope and I are sitting on the sofa, just the two of us, alone. I inch closer to her. "Last night I heard Jean-Louis tell you my life is dominated by a phantom. That's not true. A spirit visits me occasionally. Do you know about spirits?"

"You mean ghosts?" Hope looks around the room and toward the bedroom.

When she says "ghosts," I see fear on her face, hear it in her voice. Sounding like a schoolmarm, she says, "There's a ghost in the opera

Don Giovanni. And, of course, ghosts in literature—in Shakespeare's *Hamlet.* And in Toni Morrison's novel *Beloved.*" She's showing off her education again. It makes for distance between us. Still I need to explain Jean-Louis's mentioning a phantom.

"Some folks actually can communicate with spirits," I insist.

"I'm sure, but I've never known anybody in contact with the supernatural."

"You never heard about spirits and ghosts in Louisville?" I ask. "Somebody must have passed on the tales told to us when we were kids. Papa told us more than once that he'd seen the ghosts of a famous horse and his jockey, both long dead, always at midnight galloping around the track at Churchill Downs. Old folks told stories handed down from slavery about spirits of slaves, weeping and wailing, chains clanging, haunting their masters."

Hope says, "I heard that a neighbor in Louisville imagined she saw a ghost in a rocking chair on the porch of a vacant house. Black folks tell ghost stories to scare kids—and entertain them. I never took them seriously." She raises her eyebrows in a manner that seems to raise her a few inches above the fray. I'd seen that smug look on Marie.

"What about the Holy Spirit, the Holy Ghost? Do you take Him seriously?" I mean to push her buttons.

"I didn't have a clue about the Holy Ghost until I took a Bible course in college. When you study the Bible for an exam, you don't think about the spiritual meaning."

"This may be sacrilegious, but if the Holy Spirit visited people like it says in Luke 24, I believe other spirits might have visitation rights, so to speak. Anyhow I am visited by a spirit."

"Hmm. Whose?"

"Josephine Baker's."

"How do you know?" She blinks with suspicion, folds her arms across her chest, and rolls her eyes toward the ceiling.

"I can see her, hear her, talk to her. And she talks to me."

"So Josephine Baker is the phantom in your life?"

"She's a spirit, a presence, not a phantom."

"What's the difference?" Her hands are in the air, palms up. For a moment, she closes her eyes, showing me her silvered eyelids.

"A phantom is a spook that comes back to scare you, punish you for what you've done wrong. Spirits aren't like that at all. Josephine's a good spirit."

"When do you see her?" Hope switches on a more authority-than-thou voice, sounding like a doctor or a social worker. I'm sorry now that I invited her for this talk. I thought she might be a little mystical like myself. If she begins to think I'm loony, she could turn against me. That could ruin our chances for doing the show—and her feeling our kinship.

"When do I see her? Not often. The visits may be brought on by my medication." I'm backing off. I need her trust in me.

"Ah-ha, your medicine may have hallucinatory side effects."

"Maybe I ought to ask my doctor about side effects." As I say this, I'm thinking I better ask Josephine to forgive me for denying her spirit.

"What does the doctor say about your condition?"

"I need a strict diet and more exercise—what doctors always say, no matter what the problem is."

"What is the problem?"

"Diabetes. And some arthritis."

"Mom has type 2 diabetes. She's been able to control it with diet and exercise. By the way, did you mail that letter?"

"Mailed it this morning. I'll call Marie in a few days." Now I know we'll have health problems to talk about, if nothing else. "Should I tell her that her daughter has another mom?" I say jokingly.

Hope doesn't take it as a joke. Slowly she says, "If you mention it, be prepared for her reaction. She's sensitive about some family matters."

"I know." Hey, do I ever. And I'm sure our mother-daughter act will complicate things. I wonder how I'd feel if the situation were reversed.

"Hope, you should talk to her first. Tell her it's a good career move for both of us."

"I'll call her. I think she'll understand it's only to promote the show," Hope says with a shutter-speed smile that's not at all reassuring. She stands and looks steadily at me. "About your diet, what should you be eating?"

"Lots of veggies and fruits, high-fiber cereals, and cut back on fatty foods."

"It's hard to stay on that kind of diet if you eat at the café across the street," she says. André's probably told her that I'm in there everyday only having what they serve: *croque monsieur, pommes frites, sandwich au jambon.*

"I'll cook dinner for you tonight. How about it?" she says on her way into the kitchen, where she opens the frigo and immediately closes it. From the kitchen, she says, "I'll go to the *épicerie* around the corner and get some things. Anything special you'd like?"

"Whatever you choose will be OK. Let me give you some euros."

"I've got enough. I'd better hustle to get there before it closes." In a rush, Hope slams the door. I move from the sofa into the bedroom and at the window in time to see her trim figure, all in black, turn the corner. It's cool and beginning to drizzle again. She won't mind the rain, though. It won't spoil her brush cut. Still I should have given her an umbrella.

I close the window and turn to the altar. "Joséphine, *pardonne-moi mes offenses.* I know I seemed to be denying your visits. I'll find a way to show you to Hope. I felt your presence at rehearsal today. You gave me good energy. *Merci,* Joséphine." From the shelf of CDs in the living room, I take out *Josephine Baker Live at Carnegie Hall* and turn her on at full volume. I want Hope to hear Josephine when she comes up the stairs.

More than half the recording has played, and Hope's not back to hear Josephine gliding into "My Way." Waiting by the door, I wonder what could have happened. By now the *épicerie* has closed. Finally, footsteps and a knock. I open the door. Hope holding two plastic sacks bulging with groceries. André is behind her with a baguette and a bouquet of yellow roses. Instantly, in my heart, I forgive him for making off with Hope.

"André's shift was over. I invited him for dinner." Hope goes to the kitchen. André greets me with kisses and, with a courtly bow, hands me the bouquet.

Inhaling the rosy scent, I try to remember the last time a man, not counting Jean-Louis, brought me flowers. Stanley never brought flowers; he gave me cognac for special occasions.

"What a sweet thing to do, André. You've been well brought up—*bien élevé.*" I'm curious about his parents, especially his mother, French and a psychiatrist. I figure the parents are divorced. He told me his father lives in Lagos.

"Let me find something to put them in," I say, knowing I don't have a proper vase. André follows me into the kitchen where Hope is unpacking vegetables—leeks, carrots, peppers, onions, tomatoes, zucchini, and eggplants. I can't remember the last time I saw so many veggies in my kitchen.

"You planning to cook all that stuff tonight?" I'm not only questioning whether there is time to do it, but also doubting I have enough pots and pans.

"Yes, so you'll have some leftovers for tomorrow and the day after."

"Do you know what to do with leeks?" I ask.

"She makes a great leek soup. She's an excellent cook. I'm her sous-chef," André says. Ah-ha, so she's already cooked for him. He takes a carafe from the shelf above the frigo and reaches out for the roses.

"This will do as a vase," he says moving to the sink. He steps around Hope, brushing his lips across the crown of her head. Seeing them together gives me a warm, tingly sensation.

"What can I do to help?" I ask.

Unwrapping packages of cheese, Hope turns and says, "Leave the cooking to us. Put on some music and relax. Dinner will be ready in under an hour."

In the living room, again I play the CD of Josephine singing at Carnegie Hall. I stretch out on the sofa, and luxuriate in the feeling of being cared for. I hope they can hear the music over their clatter in the kitchen.

Bringing the kitchen table into the living room, André says, "Hope wants to set the table in here instead of the dining room. She likes the ambiance of this room." Singing along with Josephine, he returns with chairs.

"You know Josephine Baker's music?"

"My mother adores Josephine Baker. When I was a kid, she used to sing 'Sonny Boy' in Josephine's style like a lullaby to soothe me," he says and excuses himself to borrow some things from the café. He's gone before I can find words for what I want to ask about his mother.

Drowsy, I'm lulled to sleep by Josephine's crooning. The odor of grilled lamb wakes me up and rouses my appetite. It's like waking up in a restaurant with the table laid: ivory tablecloth, stemware, the yellow roses, and candlelight. Mouthwatering aromas flow from the kitchen. I sit up, stretch, and wipe my lids, thinking these old eyes may be playing tricks. A platter with smoked salmon and crab mousse is on the table. The promise of a tasty dinner hangs in the air. I feel like the little girl in the fairy tale who chanted a few words over a magic table that instantly produced a scrumptious meal.

Like a princess and her Prince Charming, Hope and André join me at the table. Pleased with the scene they've produced, they are all smiles. André pours the Marsannay rosé. "A detour around your diet tonight," he says with a wink.

After his toast to us and the show, I savor the salmon and crab mousse, followed by meaty lamb chops and a Niçoise ratatouille. "It's all delicious. Very tasty. Fabulous," I say more than once. After a salad and cheeses—chevre, reblochon, and roquefort—I need a pause before dessert. During dinner, we've spoken only of food, wine, and favorite Paris restaurants. André's favorite, Aux Charpentiers, was a favorite of mine when I lived on the Left Bank. Hope likes the looks of Les Papilles though she's never dined there. My favorite: Chartier on rue du Faubourg Montmartre, traditional food in a setting that reminds me of the old Paris.

"Enough about eating. I want to know what you two are up to, how you managed to hook up. It didn't look like it was going to happen."

Hope says, "I think you wanted it to happen."

"Yes, I did, but when did you click?"

"The night he took me home on his motor scooter. We went to a bar, got to know each other, talked about the usual—films, families, schools, work, and being down and out in Paris."

Turning to André, I say, "I know about Hope's family, but I don't know about yours."

"My parents met in medical school in London, where my sister was born. My father is Nigerian, so my parents moved to Lagos. My father headed a medical clinic there. Living there was difficult for my mother. She's French. She returned to France to do a psychiatry residency in Lille, where I was born. My sister and I went to schools in both places, Lagos and Lille. My parents divorced years ago." It's obvious that he's accounted for his family situation many times in his crisp English. Hardly taking a breath, he goes on. "My father married a nurse at the clinic. They have two boys."

"And your mother?"

"She has not remarried. Her work occupies her. She is in Senegal working with AIDS cases."

"And your sister?"

"Eugenia teaches at the London School of Economics. She is married to a Brit, an anthropologist."

"Interesting family." I'm wondering if Hope would feel outclassed in the company of such educated folk.

112

"And you? I know there is more to you than what we see at the café. You're some kind of artist, aren't you?"

"I'm a sculptor."

"A brilliant sculptor," Hope says.

"What did Hope tell you about her family?"

She interrupts, "We should have dessert now."

Maybe Hope doesn't want him to repeat whatever she's told him. Clearing the table, he and Hope go to and fro between the living room and kitchen. The candles, a dozen or so here and there in the room, are burning down. There may not be time this evening to learn what Hope told him, but I'd love to hear her spin on our family's story.

Hope brings a plum tart to the table. André follows her with plates. With only half of my slice eaten, I feel tipsy—drunk on food. My head drops; I snatch it back. Hope notices.

"You look sleepy. André and I'll clean up the kitchen while you get ready for bed. Okay?" She helps me get up. In the light over the bathroom mirror, I squint at my tired smile, the rehearsal makeup fading and lipstick eaten away. I bathe, brush my teeth, and in the mirror see a contented woman—of a certain age, as they say. It's been a very satisfactory day.

Undressing and getting into my nightgown, I hear their lighthearted chatter coming from the kitchen. Wishing every night could end with a fine dinner and young company, I yawn, lift my legs onto the bed, lie down, and pull up the duvet.

"We're coming in to turn out your light and say good night," Hope says in a singsong voice. She smiles at me from the foot of my bed. André, holding the carafe of roses, looks about the room and goes to the altar, where he places the roses beside the pictures of Josephine. Hope glances at the altar and says, "So that's the source of a spirit that visits." I nod and smile, too tired even to talk about Josephine.

They come to the head of the bed, Hope on one side, André on the other. Hope bends over, kisses me on the forehead, and whispers, "Good night, Violet. Sleep tight." Eyes closed, ready for sleep, in my head a choir sings: "When at night I go to sleep / Fourteen angels watch do keep / Two my head are guarding...."

14

Backstage at the Métropole, Jean-Louis is pacing the creaking floorboards in the dimly lit corridor when Hope and I arrive. We're early—half an hour early—for the three o'clock audition. He's irritated about something. "Claudine telephoned. She's been delayed," he clucks. "I should have booked a backup pianist."

"Don't worry. She'll get here on time. She's a trouper," I say to reassure him. "Hope and I can warm up without her. Can we see the studio where we'll audition?"

"Not yet. Christophe is in the studio meeting with the artistic director, Suzanne Dupont. She likes the idea of a family show, but she wants some little children in it. Children, *jamais!*" He sighs and lights a cigarette. Looking at us like a lieutenant inspecting his platoon, Jean-Louis says to Hope, "The white leotard is lovely against your skin; and the silver peplum—perfect. Silver jazz shoes—perfect." I take off my jacket so Jean-Louis can see the ankle-length, pearl gray haute couture dress he ordered for me. "The little heels with that dress look good; but please, not that print turban with the dress," he says.

"I know. I'll take off the turban before we audition." I don't like to be near him when he's tense like this.

Hope disappears and soon reappears, her smile improving my mood. "Come on stage. It's a charming house. So intimate. Seats three hundred or so," she says.

"Three hundred thirty-eight," Jean-Louis says.

We follow Hope between the blue velvet curtains onto the stage. Wood-paneled walls with gold trim surround rows of seats covered with blue velvet. The buzz of a drill draws attention to the balcony, where workmen are installing seats. Above them, the ceiling is painted with rosy, buxom female figures. In the orchestra pit, carpenters laying floorboards begin hammering.

"It is a very handsome house," Jean-Louis says.

"Great acoustics for construction, but how are they for voice?" Hope wonders. I can tell from the tap of our footsteps on the stage that the house has a good sound.

"Let's test it," I tell her. "Warm up out here." I hand my bag and jacket to Jean-Louis, who asks, "Where's the cane?"

"I don't need it today." I begin my stretching routine. Hope starts with yoga balance postures. She's a bit unsteady.

"Concentrate! Focus on one spot," I call out to her. She draws in a deep breath and on one leg stands motionless. Then together we do upper-body extensions.

The drilling and hammering workmen stop to watch.

"Four arabesques," Hope says. I think she's forgotten who her partner is. I can hardly lift my feet; lifting a leg is no longer in my repertoire. I count with her as she does them faultlessly, her body strong and supple. Looking at her makes me curse the aches of aging. How wish I were young again! I suppose I should be brimming with maternal admiration, but even true mothers must occasionally envy daughters who are graceful, vigorous, and very beautiful.

"Let's do some vocal exercises. Ready?" I ask. Her voice meets mine on the same note. She takes it higher and higher. Straining, I follow her to the upper limit of my range.

"Enough," Jean-Louis says. "Save your voices for the audition." He looks at his watch. I can tell he's worried about what to do if Claudine doesn't show up. He needs to be distracted, so I ask him who will audition us.

Pacing again, he says, "Suzanne Dupont, artistic director and a powerfully rich woman. Christophe, who is agreeable and wants to book the show; but he is new here and may not put up a strong argument. The music director, Pascal Roussel, is passionate about black singers, the concept, the entire project. Pascal and Claudine are old friends. Where is Claudine?" Jean- Louis looks at his watch. "Also the prospective underwriter, a retired industrialist from Lyon, Henri Breton. Suzanne Dupont and his late wife were childhood friends. He and Suzanne are close. She must be persuaded. You must be very motherly and Hope very daughterly, so it looks like a strong family piece—but without little children. Understand?"

"We understand. We're tight, tighter than mother and daughter," Hope says.

Tight? The family talks we've had and meals we've shared have made her feel close. Does she feel closer to me than to Marie? I mustn't think about that. For now I'm Hope's stage mother in the mood to celebrate Christmas.

Jean-Louis says, "Remember, it is a show about your merry African American Christmas."

I try to concentrate on being merry and motherly, but I'm reminded of joyless Christmases in Louisville. Year after year, the same tabletop artificial tree with a pitiful collection of presents—socks for Papa, an apron for Mama, underwear for Hampton and me; and for Marie, a big, secondhand white doll.

"*Enfin*, Claudine!" Jean-Louis shrieks, pointing to his watch. She explains that her hairdresser made her late. In their common Provence dialect they trade insults with a few understandable words: child of your father and a sheep; the goat that nursed you; son of a wild boar. Then he says in conventional French, "One hopes your head is as fresh as your hair. I like your new coiffure." At last, Claudine apologizes just as Christophe, blond, dapper, and young looking, joins us. He shakes hands all around and guides us to the backstage studio. I take Hope's arm and lean into her so my limp is less obvious.

Standing outside the studio is a matronly woman, Madame Dupont, in a peacock-blue Chanel suit. Her face is layered with powder, rouge, and eye shadow. Close to her is a stout, elderly man with a walrus mustache, Monsieur Breton. Christophe handles the introductions and tells us that we may begin when the music director arrives. Jean-Louis hands me my jacket and bag, and whispers, "I'll be waiting in the bar on the corner. *Bonne chance!* And remove the turban, please." To the group, he says he must telephone a London music hall and excuses himself. Madame Dupont turns to Monsieur Breton with a confidential whisper. Claudine, Hope and I go into the studio, a large room, bare except for four chairs near the entrance, a piano, and a bench. We put our bags and jackets on the bench. I whip off the turban and expose my head of fluffy gray hair. Hope notices and is surprised. "You hair's turned gray. It's lovely."

"My hairdresser washed out the henna. I need to look motherly," I say with a chuckle.

Claudine goes to the piano in a corner at the far end of the studio and plays a few scales. She looks pleased with the instrument. Holding on to Hope, I walk across the room and brace myself against the curve of the baby grand. I get into my diva pose, chin in the air, and gaze above the imagined audience. Hope, who has slipped on a headband with a big, white satin bow, positions herself near the center of the room. She looks poised, confident, and elegant in a white leotard and white tights.

At the door of the studio Christophe says, "We are ready to begin." He shows Madame Dupont, Monsieur Breton, and Pascal Roussel, a butterfly of a man, to their seats. Monsieur Roussel blows a kiss to Claudine, who responds with a bob of her tightly coiffed hair and closed-lipped smile.

She plays a brief medley of the songs we've rehearsed, an overture to our performance, then nods in my direction. I begin humming "The First Noel," then sing it softly and tunefully, but with a few unintentional quavers. Madame Dupont frowns and whispers to Monsieur Breton. Claudine indicates a repetition and with a crescendo and jazz beat plays the music. My body picks up the rhythm; my arms are stretched akimbo. I belt out the lyrics.

On the wall, above the auditioners, I see Josephine in her white tie and cutaway coat. She's singing along with me. When I forget the words in the second stanza, Josephine sings them through me. Tears brimming, I carefully dab my eyes with a tissue so my mascara won't run. Madame Dupont is beaming. Claudine swings into "Winter Wonderland." Hope, dancing toward me, sings the opening bars in English, then in French. We alternate lines and end it with a duet. Christophe, seated at one end, leans across the elderly pair, says something to Monsieur Roussel, who smiles and nods. But Madame Dupont is frowning again.

We pause. Hope, kneels beside me, hands folded in prayer. We sing a traditional version of "Silent Night" in French, then we do a gospel-style duet of

119

the carol in English. On "Sleep in heavenly peace," Hope bends toward me, her cheek against my breast. I look up and see Madame Dupont dabbing tears with a handkerchief.

In high spirits, Hope and I rejoice in a duet of "Go Tell It on the Mountain," like down-home African American women. Claudine remembers the tambourine and hands it to me. I shake it and pat my feet with a frenzied rhythm. Hope claps, prances, and promenades like a true believer proclaiming, "Jesus Christ is born!" The room rocks. The last piece, "Joy to the World," is Hope's solo. Singing at the top of her voice, she sways, twirls, dances. A smiling Josephine gradually fades away. Madame Dupont begins the applause while Hope, with the grace of a ballerina, is still singing of the "wonders of His love." The audition ends with our audience of four clapping enthusiastically.

According to custom, Christophe asks Hope, Claudine, and me to leave the studio so they can discuss our performance. On Hope's arm, like an aging mother supported by her daughter, I totter across the room. Madame Dupont smiles and nods to us as we leave.

In the corridor outside the studio, I heave a sigh and fall into Hope's embrace. She says, "You were awesome!"

"You and Claudine were awesome. And the spirit was with us."

"*Grace à Dieu*," Claudine murmurs. Standing near the closed door, we hear Madame Dupont's voice bubbling with excitement, but not clearly enough to make out what she's saying. Monsieur Breton says something that sounds like a question.

Christophe and Madame Dupont, speaking at the same time, seem to address the matter. Again Breton's voice. "He refuses to be the sole investor in the show," Claudine says. Madame Dupont says something in a soothing voice. Finally, they chorus, "*D'accord.*" Christophe opens the door and invites us in for another round of applause.

***

Jean-Louis has been waiting in a sleek bar around the corner from the Métropole. The place is all glass and chrome, lacking the warmth that attracts an afternoon clientele. Except for the bartender, he's alone, the ashtray in front of him heaped with cigarette butts. His expression, glazed by three or four drinks, doesn't change as Hope, Claudine, and I approach his table. Only when I speak his name does he appear alert. "Jean-Louis, we've done it. We've got the contract. And not just for three days, but for one whole week!" I'm breathless with excitement.

He makes an effort to stand and then slowly lowers himself onto the chair and crows, "You've done it! I knew you girls—pardon, I mean women— would win their hearts." Turning to the bartender, he calls, "*Champagne, monsieur!*"

"No, coffee for four," Hope orders.

"They want to meet with you tomorrow morning to work out the details, to talk about the rest of the cast," I report. "Claudine, tell him about the requirements for musicians."

Speaking their Provence dialect, Jean-Louis and Claudine reach an understanding about the musicians needed. The bartender brings coffee. We drink in the relieved silence of climbers who have narrowly escaped an avalanche. Lost in thoughts of

121

what could have gone wrong and what made the act work, we've nothing more to say until we part.

Claudine leaves first. Hope asks the bartender to call two cabs: one for Jean-Louis and the other for herself and me. Hope drops me at rue Frochot and keeps the taxi for the trip to the Tour Montparnasse, where she's working as a hostess in a new restaurant. It's an expensive ride, but, hey, we may be in the chips soon.

15

I don't get much personal mail—just bills, appeals for contributions and glossy color advertisements for sales. On returning home from the audition, I open my mailbox and find an envelope with U.S. postage and a Louisville, KY, postmark. Under the dim bulb in the vestibule, I open the envelope and read the letter.

Mrs. William J. Knox
82 Dusty Ridge Road
Louisville, KY

Sept. 30th
Dear Violetta Mae,
I received your note and had phone calls from Hope. So I decided it is time to write to you and her (a separate letter) to let you know how the news from Paris was received over here. Bill and I were happy to learn that Hope located you and that you want to be in touch with us.

Hope told you that Bill and I got married. So now I have two stepchildren, in addition to Faith and Hope. Faith is married to a very nice young man. They live near his parents in Ohio. Hope, as you must know, caught stage fever when she went away to college. She told us about the Christmas show you and she are in.

The plan you have to pass her off as your daughter troubles us greatly. We think you should drop the plan altogether. I know it may be hard for Hope to get a start in show business overseas. She needs all the help you can give her. But there must be some other way of doing it, other than pretending to be mother and daughter.

Another family matter has to do with Hampton. I wonder if you think of him as I so often do? A few years ago, Elmer Lucas paid us a visit. He told me that Hampton was in a prison camp in North Korea with him. Soviet Union officials came to the camp to brainwash prisoners. Lucas said Hampton was very impressed by their propaganda, probably went with them, and is probably living in Russia.

I wrote letters to the State Department, to senators, and to the Veterans Administration. In the form letters they sent, never was there any information or advice about how to find him. I cannot imagine how to search for a missing person in Russia. Since you are in Europe, you probably know some Russians or know an international detective service that could help us find Hampton. I surely would love to see him again.

I would like to see you again, too. Bill likes to travel. He wants to go to Paris so we can check on Hope's situation. I retired recently from teaching and he retired from horse racing, so we have time for overseas trips. Would you like us to visit you? Let us know when you write.

Yours truly,
Marie

I'm sitting on the bottom step and holding this letter when Sylvia, the gypsy fortune-teller, opens the door of her apartment. I hear her telling her pet parrot she'll be back soon. I love Sylvia's voice, a deep, dark voice with what Jean-Louis calls a Romany rumble. She closes her door and takes a few steps before she sees me. She's dressed in ordinary clothes, her brown suit, rather than the layers of loose red and orange gowns, scarves, and bangles she wears when she's working. She sees me and says, "Madame Violet, what is happening with you? You *malade*?"

"No, not sick. Just stunned by this letter from my sister. You remember, I told you about my brother, missing in action in Korea? In this letter, she says he may be alive in Russia and wants me to try to find him."

"You no go to Russia. Dangerous for you. Thieves, gunmen, kidnappers in Russia. No go to Russia. You go upstairs. I help you walk up." Sylvia's hands are under my armpits, lifting me to my feet. She's my age but strong as a sumo wrestler. With her knee under my thigh, she's behind me, moving me up the stairs. At my door, where I rummage in my purse for my key, she mumbles about Russia in French, English, and Romany. Inside, she guides me to the kitchen.

"You OK?" she asks.

"Yes, tired but OK. Excitement tires me out. "

"No go to Russia. Much excitement in Russia. Too much excitement." Sylvia seats me at the kitchen table. She turns on the overhead light and puts Marie's letter on the table before me. "Got dentist appointment at last," she says, lifting her upper lip to show space for two front teeth. Sylvia hurries out, slamming the door behind her. The noise startles Leo. He darts into the kitchen, arches his back, and stares at me with frightened eyes.

I was in Moscow once with Stanley for nearly a week. He had a gig with a big band. A few blacks were in every audience. Hampton could have been one of them. Could I have seen him and not recognized him? If he saw me, would he have known who I was?

I go back to Marie's letter. *"Since you are in Europe, you probably know some Russians or know an international detective service that could help us find Hampton.*" Marie doesn't know how big Europe is and how hard it is to trace people, especially if they don't want to be found. I could stay up late some night, go out to the corner, and ask Siberian Olga how she would find somebody in Russia. But what does she know? She's a missing person herself. Jean-Louis's friend Gérard is supposed to be able to locate people on the Internet; but if Hampton is hiding out, he's not going to be on the Internet.

"I wonder if you think of him as I so often do?" She wonders if I think of him? She hardly knew him. She was too young to know him as a playmate, a friend, a true brother. Often there's something or someone to remind me of Hampton. When I hear about horse racing, my first thought is about Hampton. When he was no more than seven years old—and I was almost nine—he showed me how to sneak into the track at Churchill. We wiggled through a hole in the fence near the entrance for horse trailers. When somebody questioned us, asked what we were doing there, Hampton always said, "We got a 'mergency message for our daddy. He works here." And we'd move along and make like we were searching for him.

When I think of my life in show business, I credit Hampton for getting me interested. He built a stage out of boards he took from an abandoned house, rounded up kids, and sold them penny tickets— stubs he'd collected at the track. Then he'd announce, "Violetta Mae is here to sing for you!" I'd shimmy onto his rickety stage, dressed in a gauzy gown I'd found in somebody's trash bin. Holding a make-believe microphone—a tin can on a stick—I'd sing a few tunes. Summertime entertainment for poor black kids.

Hampton was the one who brought that two-timing, double-dealing Pierre Prince home to meet me. And Marie wonders, do I think of Hampton?

But what to do about Hampton—and Marie? What would Josephine do? She had a half-sister and a half-brother; she brought them over to her chateau along with her mother and provided for them. I get myself out of the kitchen and into the bedroom where I light the votive candle in front of the pictures of Josephine. "Josephine, I've got to find Hampton," I tell her.

I'll ask Marie to send me what she has about Hampton. I'll need photos of him and military papers. A friendly letter to Marie may cool her jets. I'll explain that the mother-daughter show is a breakthrough chance for Hope.

I collapse on the bed. Watching the candle flickering in front of the pictures of Josephine, I think of her moving her family to France and taking on all those adopted children. If she could do all that for the sake of family, surely I can find a way to search for Hampton and reach out to Marie.

I wish I'd launched a search for him while he was writing from Korea. When he went MIA, I knew he didn't want to be found. I can understand why he'd want to lose contact with Louisville. After Papa's accident, Mama despised him. He didn't have a future at the track, and he was too proud and too smart to settle for what Louisville had to offer black men. But why give up contact with me?

I doze off, thinking of Hampton. In a dream, we are children in a downtown department store. It's not a Louisville store. It's in a big city, New York maybe. I leave the store and feel lost in the crowd on a busy street where there are shops and hotels. I step into the revolving door of a hotel. Hampton is also going around inside the door. A pane of glass separates us, but Hampton doesn't see me. We revolve, go around and around. I knock on the pane of glass. Hampton looks around, but he doesn't see me.

16

A few days after receiving Marie's letter, I'm backstage at the Métropole with Hope, Jean-Louis, Pascal Roussel, and a casting assistant. We're viewing the talent auditioning for our show. Seeing the beautiful, young people who responded to the audition call should excite me. I invited Monique and Odile. I want to work with them and some other dancers who also can sing: Karin from Guadeloupe, the Afro-Canadian Michel and another Michel from Haiti, Carla from Brazil, and two New Yorkers, Lindy and Lori. Odile's invited four Senegalese dancers. But I'm having a hard time concentrating on the parade of talent. When Jean-Louis asks what I think of someone's vocal style, I realize I'm distracted by my own thoughts: how to search for Hampton and how to answer Marie's letter.

During a coffee break, I pull Hope aside for a chat. "What do you hear from Louisville?"

"I got a letter from Mom. She's upset about the mother-daughter billing. So I phoned, talked to her about it, you know, to try to calm her. She said she wrote to you. She wants to sue the theater and sue you. She's contacted a lawyer. I'm so upset, I find it hard to focus on what we're doing."

"Me, too. I wish she would sue. It would give us some publicity. Seriously though, can you reason with her?"

"No, I can't. She's irrational where you're involved. She doesn't want me in show business. And she's threatened by you and me teaming up."

"Too bad. We're a damn good team."

"She's not going to sue. It would be silly. I'll invite her to come, see the show, and have the time of her life in Paris," Hope says.

"So she can spoil things for us during the run?" I remember her puking on my polka-dot skirt.

"She needs to see our mother-daughter act as theater. When the show ends, I'll bring her onstage and announce that she is my real mother. You and she will be drawn together because of the show."

I don't like that scenario at all, but Hope wants to reach out to Marie. So what if the public thinks I'm her mother? Let Marie deal with it in her own twisted way. Besides, I'm growing attached to the notion of having a daughter. The Métropole people say, "Will you and your daughter mind sharing a dressing room?" "There's a message on the board for your daughter." "Your daughter was here this morning." We're believable as mother and daughter.

A buzzer rings, ending the break. Returning to our seats, I whisper to Hope, "Focus on the talent. We can settle family matters later." She nods and takes her seat. Leaning forward, she looks ready to give her full attention to the next group. I try to appear involved in the auditions, but my mind is doing round-trip flights between Louisville and Moscow, worrying about what Marie will do, wondering how to locate Hampton, if he's alive.

After the auditions, Hope leaves me leaning on my cane at the taxi stand in front of the Métropole. She dashes toward the Métro to get to her Montparnasse hostess job. It's a chilly evening, typical fall weather. Watching her disappear down the subway steps, I wonder if she is warm enough in the mini-dress she wears for the hostess work. In my woolen Tyrolean jacket and pants, I'm shivering. Jean-Louis comes out of the Métropole and joins me. "We can share a taxi if you are going home. I have a rendezvous in your *quartier*," he says.

"Good. I need to talk to you."

"About the show?"

"No, about locating a missing person. My brother."

"He has been missing many years. Why try now to find him?"

A taxi pulls up and we get in. He gives the driver my address. I ask Jean-Louis if his friend, Gérard, can get information about black Americans in Russia on the Internet. He throws up his hands in a theatrical gesture of impatience. "With hundreds or maybe thousands of black Americans in Russia, you want Gérard to find your brother? He will need more indications. Or do you say clues?"

"Birth date? December 28, 1933. Born in Louisville, Kentucky, USA. Named Hampton Thomas Garfield."

"Occupation?"

"He was in the United States Army in Korea. A sergeant, I think."

"Before that?"

"He was an apprentice groom at the racetrack. He loved horses."

"*Alors*, rue Frochot already. Gérard may be able to help you. I will ask him to telephone you. You tell him the indicators," he says helping me out of the taxi.

After the taxi drives off with Jean-Louis, I look toward the corner hoping to see Olga. It's only seven-thirty, much too early for her to make an appearance. On my trek upstairs, I decide to call Marie. I'll risk a phone conversation with her to get more details about Hampton.

Settled in for the evening, comfortable in my kimono and slippers, I calculate the time difference— six hours—and place the call. I get a busy signal that I'm happy to hear. It gives me more time to think of what to say. Ten minutes later, I push the redial button. This time I get an answering machine with Marie's voice. After the beep, I leave my message:

"Hello, Marie. This is Violet calling from Paris. I know of someone who can search for missing persons. Please send me by express mail any information you have to help find Hampton. Do you have any Army documents with serial numbers and photos of him?" I pause, thinking of what else to say. The machine clicks off. I left the message and didn't even have to talk to her.

17

Jean-Louis and I are seated at a table reserved for a party of four in Aux Charpentiers on rue Mabillon. An old-fashioned bistro, it's a good choice on this chilly October evening. It was André's choice for his birthday dinner. He told us Chirac celebrated his sixtieth birthday here. Treating Hope and André to dinner was my idea.

The maître d'hôtel and waiters greeted us like we're frequent clients. An oversized ice bucket with half a dozen bottles of champagne at one end of the bar was welcoming, too. White tablecloths on rows of tables and flower-shaped ceiling lights brighten the room. Several tables are occupied by couples with scholarly Left Bank looks. Pointing to carpenters' models of steeples and towers on the walls, Jean-Louis says, "Those were built more than a century ago when members of the carpenters' union dined here. It is a restaurant that respects history, a suitable place for a birthday dinner."

A party of eight is shown to a narrow staircase leading to a downstairs dining room. Beyond the stairs, the open kitchen door affords a glimpse of *le chef cuisinier* and his staff. The aroma of hearty bistro food overtakes me: *gratinée, escargots, agneau rôti, boeuf bourguignon, boudin noir, magret de canard.* The anticipation of good food is comforting; but Jean-Louis's discomfort is obvious.

"Jean-Louis, you ought to be jumping for joy. You negotiated a good contract, found a great supporting cast and talented musicians. Rehearsals are going well. You're making a fantastic come back in the business. So why are you gloomy?"

"I am lost without Boris."

"I miss him, too, but you may find another Russian wolfhound. Speaking of Russia, has your friend Gérard made any progress in the search for my brother? I gave him a description of Hampton nearly two weeks ago; and last week I sent him the documents and pictures my sister mailed."

"Did he not tell you? He has information about four such men, black Americans, formerly in the Army, between seventy and eighty-five years old, living in or near Moscow."

"One of them has got to be Hampton!" I exclaim, pounding a fist on the table.

"Perhaps, but Gérard wants to be certain to find the right one."

A waiter hands us menus and pauses a moment before asking if we would like *apéritifs.* "Vodka, *s'il vous plait,*" Jean-Louis says. I order a Perrier.

"There may be more than four. Gérard is still searching, searching in other Russian cities. Patience. Your brother has been missing for how many years? And overnight you want to locate him? Why do you hurry now?"

"I'm in a hurry because Hampton, if he's alive, and I are in the autumn of life. You get what I mean? And winter is coming on fast and hard."

"I know the autumn of life, to be sure," he says, and shifts from gloomy to glum.

The waiter brings our drinks. We lift the glasses and together say, "*Santé.*"

Jean-Louis adds, "To memories of Boris."

And I say, "To finding Hampton alive and well."

At the door, a young couple waits to be ushered to a table. Behind them, a party of five, a family—a midlife couple, their adult son (whose profile duplicates the father's), and two teenage daughters. Then in comes a middle-aged man in a rumpled gray suit with *Le Monde* for company. The restaurant is filling up, and I haven't heard the sputter of André's motor scooter arriving with Hope.

"I wonder what's delayed them?" I ask to fill the silence.

"Sex, sex, and variations on sex. Oh, to be young again, for just a few weeks," Jean-Louis says, his eyes closed to picture himself on what he calls his "screen of memories."

At that moment, Hope and André appear at the entrance. André spots us and guides Hope to the table. Between kisses for me and Jean-Louis, she apologizes. "We're late because we came by bus. It was slower than the scooter." André shakes hands with Jean-Louis and kisses me. "Sorry to have kept you waiting," he says.

The bus trip must have heightened their appetites. Immediately they survey the menu. André orders a '99 Chassagne-Montrachet. The waiter nods his approval. Dinner is on me, so I'm paying more attention to the prices than usual. With little delay, we have the first course: *escargots* for André and me; *saumon fumé* for Hope and Jean-Louis, whose mood improves as he begins to eat. Jean-Louis makes small talk with Hope about how well the rehearsals are going. She likes working with Pascal, the music director. Jean-Louis says he adores all the dancers, not merely the three young men in the company. I confess I worry constantly about looking lively in the midst of the youthful energy that surrounds me onstage.

André, who fancies himself a wine expert, tells us we should be tasting ripe fruit flavors in the wine. During the second course, I'm putting away a delicious *magret de canard* when Jean-Louis turns to Hope and says, "We were talking about your Uncle

135

Hampton before you came. What do you know about him?"

Hope hesitates, as if trying to recall what she may have heard about Hampton, before saying, "I never knew him. He was declared missing before I was born. Mom wrote letters to government agencies about him. She was told relatives might be entitled to his GI life insurance, but he wasn't declared dead. After a while she stopped making inquiries about him."

Was it the money Marie was after? I almost choke on a mouthful of duck. I sip some wine before saying, "So Marie just wants to find out if he's alive." If I sound put out, it's because I am. Marie is devious. I suppose Hope knows that. Daughters know the dark sides of their mothers' character.

"Gérard is searching for him. He is able to locate people by Internet," Jean-Louis says.

"He may be difficult to find," André says. "Some people change their names, take on new identities in exile."

"But he can't change his skin color," I remark. "Blacks are easy to spot in Russia. When I was in Moscow with Stanley, we saw very few blacks. Some were African students, mostly men. We always nodded or shook hands with them, even if we didn't have a common language. They looked lonely."

"If Uncle Hampton is alive, he may not want to be found. What if he's been accused of desertion? Or spying? Searching for him may not be in his best interest," Hope says."

André, finishing his *boeuf bourguignon*, agrees. "Exposing him could derail the course of his life. You need to be very cautious. I hope your agent is discreet."

"I assure you, Gérard is extremely discreet," Jean-Louis says in his patronizing tone. I've lost interest in the duck, now deep in thoughts of "what ifs." What if we find Hampton? What if he doesn't want anything to do with Marie and me? What if he's faced with criminal charges? What if we learn he's dead? These unspoken questions silence me for a while.

"This is heavy stuff. We ought to lighten up. After all, it's a birthday party," I finally say. "If everybody's finished, let's go to my place for dessert and champagne." My invitation isn't a surprise. Hope had a cake delivered this morning; and yesterday André deposited a bottle of Veuve Clicquot in my frigo. The bill paid, the maître d'hôtel and waiters give us a warm send-off. Jean-Louis phones for a taxi; minutes after we step outside our taxi arrives.

In my dining room, where Hope has set the table, we gather around the birthday cake with twenty-eight candles. Singing "*Bon Anniversaire*" and "Happy Birthday" to André and several toasts do little to lighten the mood. André mentions a Nigerian friend in exile who telephoned birthday greetings from London.

Hope asks me, "Do you think of yourself as being an exile?"

"I'm not an exile, not an escapee from a political crisis. I'm an expatriate. There's a difference. I wasn't forced to leave the States. When I left, I was ready for a lucky break, a different scene. I was attracted to Paris because of the recognition Josephine Baker had received here, and the goodwill and attention given to other black artists over the years. I live in Paris because I like the way I'm treated here. I'm treated with respect. Nobody here has ever told me I couldn't do something because of my skin color. Nobody here has ever called me 'nigger.'" Hope and André exchange glances with eyebrows raised.

"We've run into racism in Paris, as have most of our black friends," André says.

"It never used to be so. Paris once was a place where blacks could count on decent treatment," I tell them.

"When you came in the early fifties, blacks were exotic strangers. The French welcomed the few who visited and those who stayed, especially if you were a black American," Hope says. "They were anxious to show France as much more tolerant, fraternal, and egalitarian than the States. But attitudes of the French changed with the increase in black immigration from their former colonies in West Africa and the Caribbean."

"As for decent treatment," André says, "just look at the racial composition of the labor force, the makeup of the National Assembly and major political parties, corporations and unions in France. You must admit racialist attitudes here operate against the advancement of people of color. France needs a civil-rights movement and an affirmative-action program."

"You left America before the Civil Rights Movement changed things. Since you left, there has been substantial progress," Hope says.

"I'm sure a lot of black folks in the States still don't have decent housing, safe neighborhoods, or good schools," I tell them.

"There are a lot of blacks and Arabs in Paris suburbs where living conditions are deplorable and schools are inferior," André insists.

"The demonstrations and fires in the suburbs have been protests about poor living conditions," Jean-Louis says.

"And Sarkozy called the kids protesting 'scum,'" Hope says.

"I know that. I read the papers and listen to the news. But I also know blacks in the States struggle with their slave history and poor blacks with the added disgrace of poverty." I pause for a moment before continuing. "Still, I'd rather live here. Life in Paris is more civil, more agreeable than places I know in the States. Years ago I saw the bumper sticker: 'America—love it or leave it!' Well, I left. And I've got no regrets."

"So you are not in accord with Josephine Baker's '*J'ai Deux Amours*'—two loves, your country and Paris," Jean-Louis says.

"She changed her tune, didn't she? Changed one word, and began singing, '*Mon pays est Paris*'—'My country is Paris.'" As if on cue, I hear Josephine humming her theme song. At first I think it's in my head, but Hope looks around as if she hears something, too. I get up and go to the bedroom. Surrounded by a pale blue aura above the altar, Josephine, in a simple white gown, is softly singing: *J'ai deux amours, / Mon pays est Paris / Par eux toujours, / Mon coeur est ravi.* She repeats it and I sing the stanza with her, but I'm singing "*J'ai un amour.*" She smiles and the aura vanishes, but her fragrance lingers.

I return to the party. Jean-Louis, holding Leo on his lap absentmindedly strokes him. Hope and André give me the strangest looks. Hope says, "The singing—it didn't sound like your usual voice."

"I was singing along with Josephine. She came for a visit. Like she knew we were talking about her, France, and the States."

Hope and André exchange glances. Hope says to me, "You must be very tired. Or perhaps it's your medication."

André stands and reaches for Hope's hand. "It's late," he says, "and time to go." Jean-Louis gently lowers Leo to the floor and prepares to leave. The party is over. My guests are departing with renewed concern about my state of mind. Hope says, "May I help you get ready for bed?"

"No, thanks," I say rather sharply. I see them to the door. On the dining room table, Leo licks the plates clean. I cover the cake and cork the champagne. On my way to bed, I stop in front of the altar, look at the pictures of Josephine, and think of the search for Hampton. I doubt he's alive. The men in our family never lived much beyond sixty. And I wonder if Josephine would search for somebody who's been missing for half a century.

18

A few days later while I am having coffee with Hope at the café, André brings her his portable phone and tells Hope she has a call. She takes the phone and goes to a corner near the café door, her back to the table where I'm sitting. Moments later, she says, "*Elle parle à elle-meme...pense qu'elle voit les fantômes...*" She talks to herself...thinks she sees ghosts. I'm eavesdropping. I suppose she thinks I can't hear her over the chatter of habitués at the bar. She listens, nods a few times. "*Pouvez-vous m'indiquer un médecin?*" she asks. Can you recommend a doctor? A long pause on her end, more nodding. She laughs nervously, then says, "*Au revoir,*" and presses the button turning the phone off. She goes to the bar, hands the phone to André, and comes back to our table where her coffee, by now, is cold.

"The phone call—was that one of your girlfriends?"

"No, it was André's mother. Calling about her mail, the apartment, and stuff. She's still in Senegal." Her fingers ripple around her head and come together in her lap. She's looking steadily into my eyes. Is she going to tell me what that call really was about? She must know I've overheard something. I'm waiting.

She sips some coffee, and then says, "I was telling her about a friend who ought to see a doctor. A young friend, a dancer who may be pregnant."

Liar. I'm mulling over how to say I know she's lying. Then I wonder about my hearing. Did I hear her correctly? Am I going paranoid? "What are your friend's symptoms?" I ask.

Flustered, guilt all over her face, she says, "There's no pregnant friend. I told her I'm concerned about you. She's a doctor with good connections and..."

"You told me she's a shrink. You think I need to have my head examined, don't you? Well, maybe I am crazy—crazy for trying to share my life with you." Anger zigzags through me like a lightning bolt.

"Violet, please. I'm worried about your health."

"My mental health is good, thank you."

"Talking to dead people isn't healthy."

"Maybe the dead are better company than the living. Kinder. Less likely to stir up doubts about my sanity."

She looks embarrassed. "But they're not here to care for you. You need to visit a clinic, see a doctor."

"I have a doctor—Dr. Chang. If anything is wrong with my mind, he'd know about it. I don't want to talk about this anymore. And I don't want you talking about my mental state with anybody—not with Jean-Louis, André, or his shrink of a mother. Understand?" I push away from the table, put on my raincoat, get my cane, and start to leave. But my knees are wobbly, like they've turned to jelly. I feel lightheaded and suddenly weak. I hear somebody say, "*Elle va tomber!*" She's going to fall! I turn to see who's falling. I feel somebody's weight under me, arms holding me as I slip to the floor.

***

Waking up in a hospital bed, no recollection of how I got here is frightening. Like losing my place in the lyrics of a song, forgetting the words, but worse. A needle in my arm is connected to a transparent tube attached to a bottle of fluid hanging above the bed. Something serious happened. Diabetic coma? Did I forget to take my medicine? A stroke? I had the feeling of falling. Did I fall off the stage, fall into the

142

orchestra pit? I move my feet, ankles, legs. Nothing hurts. No bones broken.

Voices outside the room: Hope's voice and the voice of another woman speaking English. So Hope's brought me here. Had me committed. She thinks I'm nuts because I sing with Josephine. Hope's turned against me. Joined forces with Marie. I hear a man's voice. It sounds like Dr. Chang. Lord, let it be Chang.

A prayer answered. Dr. Chang comes to my bedside and strokes my arm, the arm not hosting the needle. "Madame Fields, how are you feeling?"

"Confused. I'm in a hospital, and I don't know how I got here or why I'm here."

In his direct, no-nonsense tone, Chang says, "You fainted in a café. You were brought here to the American Hospital by ambulance. Your niece accompanied you. You were unconscious on arrival but quickly regained consciousness. Your vital signs are normal. Nothing remarkable has been detected so far. It looks like a typical case of exhaustion."

A stout, freckled, red-haired nurse looks at me from the foot of the bed. She says slowly in a British accent, "Your niece, Miss Grayson, is waiting outside."

Chang continues, "Your niece told me that you are preparing a Christmas show. The rehearsals require vigorous activity, not at all part of your normal routine. That might account for this episode. I don't think it's serious, but I want you to spend two days here so we can do some tests. Miss Swindon will be your nurse. I'm on call this weekend, so I'll be around if you need me."

"What kind of tests are you doing?" I move my legs to be sure they are still attached.

"An electrocardiogram and some other routine measures."

"You think I've got heart problems?"

"While you're here, we ought to get baseline data on you, that's all. I'll review your prescriptions. Your niece suggested side effects from a medication. If anything is irregular, I'll let you know. If you need me, I'll be on this floor for an hour or so," Chang says on his way out.

The scene in the café is coming back to me. Hope was on the phone talking to André's mother, telling her I'm imagining things. I suppose Hope has told Dr. Chang that I talk to spirits. I know they've got a psychiatric wing here. I'd better be alert as to where I am and where they want to put me.

"Your niece wants to see you," Miss Swindon says while taking my blood pressure.

"I'm too tired to talk to her."

"Your pressure is normal, but I'll tell her not to stay long." Miss Swindon leaves and, in the corridor, has a few words with Hope. Moments later, Hope, at the foot of the bed, is giving me a last-rites look. Her forehead is furrowed with worry. I feel sorry for her. At the same time, I know I'm in here because of her. It was that phone call that knocked me off my feet. I pretend to be groggy, too tired for a visit.

"Aunt Violet, how are you?" she coos in her ingénue voice.

I've told her to drop the "aunt." With my eyelids at half-mast, I say in a hoarse whisper, "I'm going to be okay. Out in two days and back in rehearsals. Tell them they can count on me. But just now, I'm very sleepy." I yawn and close my eyes as if I'm dozing off.

"The nurse said you're exhausted, so I'm not going to stay." She turns to a chair where she's placed her coat and umbrella. Putting on her coat, she asks anxiously, "Can I bring you something? Fruit? Magazines? A radio? What will you need?"

"Rest, that's all." Then I think of Leo. "Feed Leo. Sylvia the fortune-teller has a key to my place. And Jean-Louis has a key. And while you're there, please water the plants."

"Don't worry. I'll take care of everything. Get some sleep. I'll come back this evening."

"Come tomorrow. Not this evening." Wondering if I'm being too theatrical, I begin to drift off. Hope tiptoes out. The injection they gave me to help me rest is working. No longer pretending, I'm out like a light.

***

The clatter of a cart wakes me up. Someone is calling, "Madame Fields. Violet Fields. Violet, it's time for pills and *petit déjeuner*." The woman gives my name an Antilles lilt. I look around to get my bearings. It's a hospital room with a view of dark clouds in the morning sky, raindrops on the window, limp, brown leaves in the treetops. The streets are probably slippery, puddles everywhere. I'd just as well be in the hospital in weather like this.

Fully awake, now I'm restless and anxious. What happens to my role in the show if they keep me here? Have things soured with Hope? To search or not to search for Hampton? How to handle Marie? I'm helpless here, unable to do anything about the show or the family or myself. I need to get out of this place.

I reach for the phone on the bedside stand to call Jean-Louis. The line is dead. I drop the receiver noisily. A hospital aide, with a smile born and bred in the Antilles, says, "That phone won't work until you pay, Madame." Her manicured hands—hands the color of mine—smooth the blanket and fluff the pillows. She pushes a button that raises the head of the bed so that I'm sitting up. She asks if I am comfortable. Despite the confusion in my head and

145

conflicts in my heart, "Yes, thanks. Except for this needle in my arm, I feel fine."

"We have tea or coffee," the aide says as she places before me a tray with an apricot compote, yogurt, brioche, butter, and strawberry jam. I could be in a spa with such room service. I need a little pampering, not just rest. I eat the brioche, have some coffee, and fall asleep.

Miss Swindon wakes me up telling me in her Queen's English that I'll be taken to the EKG unit. By the time I've made sense of the letters, someone is rolling my bed down the hall to an elevator. On another floor, in a room with panels of dials and wires, a technician explains what she's doing as she lubricates spots on my chest. She attaches electrodes, zaps me, and before I can ask about the condition of my heart, I'm rolled back to my room.

At first, I think I've been taken to the wrong room. Four bouquets of flowers are on the windowsill; on the bedside stand is a cellophane-wrapped basket of bananas. I take the card from the bananas: "From Josephine and Jean-Louis with affection." Propped up in bed, the card in my hand, I'm rocking with laughter when Jean-Louis comes in.

"Being in hospital has made you merry," he says.

"No, it's the basket of bananas from you and Josephine!" My cheeks are wet with tears of laughter.

"They have arrived already? I thought the card would amuse you. But how are you?" His voice turns serious. He's genuinely worried about me.

"The doctor says I'm exhausted. I've been tired lately, but to the point of exhaustion?"

"Fatigue and stress about your family. But I have good news. It may reduce your stress. Gérard has identified someone, probably your brother. Same birth date. Lives in a Moscow suburb." Jean-Louis takes off his raincoat, and from the breast pocket of his blazer, he takes out a paper and reads, "Tomas Mikhail Grischevich, horse trainer and breeder; breeds Arabians for export. Co-proprietor of a horse farm. Travels to auctions and horse shows in Germany, Czech Republic, and Ukraine. Knows American English and Korean. Of African descent; born 28 December 1933; height: one meter seventy-seven; weight: seventy-two kilograms. Widowed, three children." He hands me the paper. I read the description.

"It's got to be Hampton! How did Gérard get all this from the Internet?"

"Horses. That was the key indicator."

"Can he get an address? A phone number?"

"He has an e-mail address for Grischevich. But are you sure you want to make contact? Hope and André warned about risks. Gérard, however, thinks it is safe to contact him. The Cold War is over. Russia and America have rapport. Nobody cares to prosecute or persecute now."

"Hampton's alive! Sure, I want to contact him." I'm excited and nervous about what the next round of news will bring. What if he doesn't want to know me? Or what if he's an imposter, some black dude who stole Hampton's identity documents?

"I shouldn't get my hopes up. It may not be Hampton after all."

"If it is your brother, what about the consequences for him? He has a business and children."

"In the States, there was a radio game show called Truth or Consequences. Well, I want the truth. If it's Hampton, I want to talk to him, tell him how I've missed him. We'll just have to take the consequences."

Trying to slide off the bed, I'm held back by the tube with intravenous drips. As if he knows I want to make a getaway, Dr. Chang appears and says sternly, "Madame Fields, I want you to remain in bed." In no-nonsense French, he asks Jean-Louis to leave the room for a few minutes.

Looking at his watch, Jean-Louis says, "I must leave anyhow to meet Gérard for *déjeuner*. I will tell him to contact Tomas Grischevich, send him your press kit, and tell Grischevich you are in hospital. That should get a reply. He either knows you or does not. *À bientôt*."

Miss Swindon comes in, closes the door, and assists Dr. Chang, visiting regions of my body uninhabited for years. Scarcely following their itinerary below my waist, I'm thinking of what to say and do if Tomas Grischevich is Hampton.

***

The last time I saw Hampton was at Papa's funeral in 1950. He was going on seventeen, a skinny, bowlegged kid, with big, sorrowful, dark eyes. Miserable when he met me at the Louisville train station, he was shaking with grief. He drove me straight to the funeral parlor in Papa's old Ford. On the way, Hampton told me that Papa was showing him how to break a rambunctious horse when the horse bucked and threw him. Papa let out a cry heard all around the track. The horses in the stalls got stirred up. Seeing Papa thrown, Hampton forgot to latch the stall of the horse he had been handling. The horse broke out of its stall. Papa was lying on the ground injured. The horse trampled Papa. A hoof broke his skull. He died instantly. Everybody at the track knew that Hampton had been working with the horse that killed Papa.

The burden of guilt made Hampton droop. He didn't look sixteen; he looked like a crumpled, old man. He said Mama told him he was to blame for what happened. She said if Hampton weren't her son, she'd want him tried for manslaughter.

Hampton didn't want to go to Papa's funeral. Mama made him go. I heard her say he had to face the "misfortune" he'd caused. Hampton cried throughout the church service and the burial.

The last time I saw Hampton, he was crying. I understood why Hampton left Louisville to join the Army—to escape. And he probably chose to go missing in action.

***

Completing his tour of my organs, Dr. Chang says, "Except for the fainting, your condition hasn't changed since I saw you last. The EKG was normal. We need to do a CAT scan before I can release you." He explains that a CAT scan will show images of the inside of my body. "If you have a small tumor, for example, the scan is likely to reveal it."

"As if I don't already have enough on my mind, you want me to worry about something growing in my body?"

"Madame Fields, I don't expect to find a tumor. It was just an example." He gives me a reassuring pat on the shoulder, and then writes something on my chart. When he and Miss Swindon leave, I start scanning myself, feeling here and there for lumps.

A little later, the aide from the Antilles comes in singing, "*Déjeuner, Madame.*" She's pushing a trolley with aromas that would arouse an anorexic's appetite. On my bedside stand, she places a tray with a grilled lamb chop, green beans, and potatoes au gratin.

"I'm not very hungry," I say, turning away from the tray.

"Madame, you must eat. Regain your strength."

"Call me Violet. What's your name?"

"Félicité."

"A lovely name. Félicité, I want to know who sent me flowers. The card on the bouquet of yellow and gold pom-pom chrysanthemums, what does it say?"

"'To Violet: Our best wishes for a prompt recovery. Suzanne Dupont and Henri Breton.'"

"And that huge arrangement of...are they lilies?"

"Amaryllis, Madame. The card says: 'Dearest Violet, Please get well soon. The show cannot go on without you. With affectionate best wishes, The Cast of *Les Belles de Noël* and the Métropole Staff.'"

"And the bunch of violets. I should know violets, don't you think?"

"'To Aunt Violet, Blessings and best wishes for a rapid recovery. I love you! Yours always, Hope.'"

"May I see that last card, the one you just read?" Félicité gives me the card. I look at it and start crying.

"You must be very close to your niece," she says, giving me a box of tissues.

"She's like a daughter to me," I sob.

With a hint of envy in her voice, she says, "You are lucky to have her in Paris near you." I assume she probably has sons and daughters on the other side of the Atlantic. The thought humbles me.

"I don't feel like eating. Please take away the tray." Félicité reaches for the tray.

"Wait a minute. What's the dessert?"

She removes the cover of a bowl and says, "Plum compote with *crème fraîche*."

"I want the dessert, but take the rest away." Félicité leaves the compote and leaves me holding

Hope's message against my breast. I'm back and forth about Hope, sometimes thinking the world of her and sometimes thinking the worst. If only I could let myself wholeheartedly trust her.

***

"Nap time is over, Madame Fields. Try to look perky. You have visitors," Miss Swindon chirps. She hands me a glass of apple juice and pushes the button that raises my bed so that I'm sitting up. I hear voices outside, probably a medical team bent on finding something inside me that they can call "remarkable." I drink the juice and put on my welcome smile.

At the door, Miss Swindon says, "You may come in now."

Jean-Louis and Hope come in, followed by the entire company of *Les Belles de Noël*—singers, dancers, and musicians. Twenty young people plus Jean-Louis, greeting me with hugs, kisses, waves, salutes, and well wishes, crowd into the room.

I can't believe it. Everybody has turned up! "So you've come here to rehearse?"

"We reported for the rehearsal, but we were too depressed by your absence." Monique says sadly.

"Instead of rehearsing, here we are," Odile says, "We have a new dance routine to accompany 'Joy to the World,' but not enough space here to dance."

"We all know the arrangement. Let's sing it," Hope says. She lifts her arms like a conductor and leads them in a rollicking gospel version of the carol. I'm sure they can be heard throughout the hospital. Singing, clapping, and swaying with the rhythm, I'm ecstatic and proud to have them all around me. When they finish, there's a burst of applause from the staff and patients gathered outside the room.

151

"Sing 'Winter Wonderland,'" Jean-Louis proposes, but Miss Swindon closes the performance with a brusque, "That will be all, thank you. Thank you for coming." The company trickles out, offering get-well wishes, blowing kisses, saying *à bientôt*.

Hope stays with me. "I knew our visit would give you a boost," she says with satisfaction. "By the way, I have news from Mom. I called her, told her that you've suffered exhaustion and are in the hospital. She was sorry to hear it. I urged her to come to Paris to see you and to see the show. She said they might come. What do you think of that?"

"What about her wanting to sue?"

"She's under the impression that you won't be able to perform."

"Well, she's mistaken. I'll be back to work in a few days. By the way, I heard you talking about me to André's mother. That really upset me. Then you sent those violets with your message about love. Thinking somebody is mental, and talking about it, not with the person—in this case, me—but with somebody else, who doesn't even know me—is that how you show your love?"

"I needed advice. She recommended a psychiatrist from Haiti, Dr. Marcel Desrochers. He specializes in people who communicate with spirits. I saw him yesterday and told him about you."

"And just what did you tell him?"

"What you said about Josephine and what Jean-Louis said about you. The doctor said some people have channels through which they can receive spirits. Typically they are highly perceptive women with better access to supernatural circulation than ordinary people. He said I shouldn't be at all concerned about your mental state, if you manage your life rationally." She pauses, then says very slowly and thoughtfully, "He implied that since I've heard some rustling and singing, and smelled something in the air when your Josephine was around, I may have the capacity for channeling spirits, too. So we may have even more in common than I thought."

"Did he wipe away your doubts about my mind?"

"Yes, but he raised some questions about my own," Hope says with nervous laughter.

"You've got a lifetime to find answers to such questions. Come, let me give you a hug. I'm sorry for thinking the worst." My arms are outstretched to embrace Hope. Miss Swindon chooses this moment to come in.

"The CAT scan technician can see you right now, Madame Fields." To Hope she says, "You may want to wait. She'll be back in half an hour."

"I'll come back tomorrow morning," Hope says. I'm still holding on to Hope, holding her hand, when an aide arrives to take me to the CAT scan unit.

19

I'm finishing breakfast when Dr. Chang makes his morning visit. "All the tests look normal, Miss Fields. I'm going to release you today," Chang says. "Remember, you must pay close attention to your diet and daily medications. I understand your niece will escort you home. Your next appointment is in mid-January. Take better care of yourself." He gives me a vigorous handshake.

A few minutes after he leaves, Félicité comes in. She finds me in the closet looking at what I was wearing when they brought me in.

"Do you want help getting dressed?" Félicité asks.

"No, thanks, I can dress myself." I don't want her to see my ragged bra and faded underpants, soup-stained sweatshirt and baggy gray pants. Dingy, white socks are stuffed in my old, brown loafers. And my raincoat, a man's Burberry, left at our place years ago by one of Stanley's cronies. I look out the window. Clear, blue sky. I won't need the raincoat today.

Félicité leaves me alone to struggle into my clothes. I glance at myself in the full-length mirror inside the closet door. My hair's a mess. I'm a fright.

I'm hardly dressed when Félicité returns and says, "Madame, take off those clothes. Your niece is here with some clothes for you."

Hope, right behind her, says, "I think you'll like the Chanel suit Suzanne Dupont sent. She never wore it. It's too small for her. The color—it's called celadon this season—is good on you." Like a magician pulling rabbits out of a hat, she pulls one accessory after another out of the suitcase she's brought. "I found a handbag to match. These green sling-backs and this scarf were in your armoire."

"*Très jolie*," says Félicité, pulling off my sweatshirt. She and Hope dress me as if I'm their doll. Hope rouges my cheeks, powders my face, and applies eyeliner and lipstick. Félicité brushes my hair into an upswept mini-afro. I gaze at myself in the mirror. The change is amazing.

"Now you're ready for the photographers," Hope says.

"What photographers?" I ask.

"Jean-Louis sent a press release to the media. He and Monsieur Breton are in the lobby, along with eight or ten photographers and a TV camera crew. Lean on my arm so you won't need the cane," Hope says.

Carrying the suitcase and my cane, Félicité says, "If photographers are waiting, Dr. Chang and Nurse Swindon should be pictured with you. I'll page them."

"Good idea," says Hope, who, like a stage director, is preparing me for a scene. She herself is wearing stage makeup and a miniskirt that shows off her legs. I begin to get the idea.

Early the next morning—just after ten—I am just getting up when Jean-Louis arrives at my apartment with a bundle of newspapers. Moments later, Hope comes with copies of the same papers, turned to pages with our pictures. Our photos are in the tabloids. In the photos, Hope and I are in the center flanked by Breton and Chang. I translate the captions and read: "Violet Fields Goes from Hospital to Music Hall;" "American Mother-Daughter

Teamwork;" "Violet Fields Recovers to Make Comeback."

"Take off your coats. Come, let's sit down to take this all in," I say, leading them into the dining room. Seated at the dining table on my rickety chairs, slip-covered by that trio of decorating clowns, Hope, Jean-Louis, and I pass the newspapers around, commenting on statements about our forthcoming show.

"Your hospitalization was timed impeccably," Jean-Louis boasts, as if we'd planned it. "The news hits the papers today—the holiday, *Toussaint*. People are at home reading about you. I am sure Monsieur Breton is elated about the publicity."

"You seem elated, too," Hope says.

"Yes, but we must keep the attention of the press. I can alert the photographers, if you and André will stage a fight in the street," Jean-Louis proposes.

"No," Hope says, "we don't do that sort of thing—in public."

"What about nude photos, Hope, for a sexy magazine?" he asks, knowing how she'll respond.

"Never!" Hope snarls with a mean stare.

"What about nude photos of me? Have you thought of that, Jean-Louis?" I say.

"Try to be serious. We need good ideas for stories. Your family story—two mothers and their daughter, Hope. The entire story can be told after the show ends. If Gérard receives a reply from Russia and if the man is your brother, *alors*, there will be sensational story material."

"No reply yet?"

"Patience, Violetta."

"What have you heard from Faith?" I ask Hope.

"I haven't contacted her yet," she admits.

"And you've been on my case about patching things up with Marie. Call her today. Not now. It's not yet dawn in Cleveland. Invite her and her husband to come for the opening. I want to meet this Greenberg dude."

Jean-Louis says, "Invite them for the closing. The show has a short run. It needs a night or two to shake it down. The last performance will be the best. The cast party after the closing will be a celebration. Your family will attend the party. Then we reveal the mother-daughter and aunt-niece story, and announce the next show, your Easter gospel program."

"We need more publicity for Hope. The next generation has to carry on the tradition. Our great bronze Hope," I say. Hope flashes her big Garfield smile.

"Yes, a slick, promotion story about Hope, launching her as a rising star," crows Jean-Louis, standing with an air of tail feathers fluttering. He looks at his watch. "I have a rendezvous for *déjeuner* with Dupont and Breton. I will speak to them about an Easter show. Violetta, *repose-toi*. You must not exert yourself." After kisses for us both, Jean-Louis is out the door.

"It's strange to see Jean-Louis leave without Boris following him," I say quietly, almost to myself.

"Let's get another Russian wolfhound for him," Hope says.

"Great idea! Same coloring, a well-trained, mature dog. Not a puppy. Jean-Louis can't deal with a frisky pet."

"I'll get André to help me find another Boris."

"How is André?"

"At the moment, he's irritated with me."

"What's wrong?"

"He wants me to move in with him, but I'm not ready for that kind of commitment. I have to vacate his mother's place next week. She's coming back from Senegal," Hope says. She hesitates, as if she's going to ask what I want her to ask of me. Instead, she says, "I must buy a present for her."

And so I ask, "Why don't you come and live with me for a while? The sofa is convertible. And there's space in the living room armoire for your things."

Close to tears, she says, "I thought you'd never ask. I'd like to try living with you, if you wouldn't find me in the way."

"You know that living with me also means living with Josephine, too."

"Don't forget Leo. I think I can handle the scene."

"I'd love to have your company," I say.

She holds up an open palm, and I slap her a high five. " It's a deal," she says.

"You'll need a key. Get my key from Sylvia the fortune-teller."

Hope is on her feet smiling down at me. She bends and kisses tears on my cheeks. She says, "I can move in tomorrow, if that's not too soon."

"It's not soon enough," I sigh with relief.

She goes to the foyer where she's hung her coat on the rack; the door closes and she's gone. I fold and neatly stack the newspapers and sit here thinking, I've been blessed with a niece who cares for me, who wants to come and live with me.

20

After two days at home, I was eager to be back at the Métropole. Rehearsal didn't go well today. The music director had a migraine headache, the drummer didn't show up, Odile was late, and Monique and Carla the Brazilian had the giggles. And Hope was distracted; she missed several cues. It's been a frustrating afternoon.

As I'm leaving the Métropole, a taxi pulls up and out steps Jean-Louis, calling my name and waving an envelope. He says, without kisses or even a bonjour, "I have Grischevich's reply!"

"I can't read here in the street. It's too windy. Let's go across the street to the tea salon." I take his arm as we cross on the zebra stripes. Cars are coming thick and fast. I lift my cane in the air to signal the traffic to slow down.

Four of the five tables in the salon are taken. Two gray ladies—gray haired and in gray coats—are at my favorite table near the window. Our only choice is the tiny table in the rear. "Mint tea for both of us," Jean-Louis tells the waiter.

Warm from rehearsing, I slip out of my Tyrolean jacket. Still in his fedora and overcoat, Jean-Louis takes a sheet of paper from the envelope.

"Tomas Mikhail Grischevich responded to Gérard by e-mail." He shows me the message I read it aloud: "'I had two sisters: Violetta Mae Garfield and Marie Ann Garfield. I knew of a Violet Fields in Paris. I cannot assist with her search for Hampton Thomas Garfield until she provides further information and evidence of identity."

"Hey, it's him. It's Hampton. I can easily prove I'm Violetta Mae and Violet. But he's being very cautious, like he's scared of something or somebody."

"He may think it is a CIA trap. Desertion could be a problem for him. America can still request extradition of military deserters, according to Gérard. In any case, he may not reveal himself until you prove you are Violetta Mae Garfield."

"Don't my photos prove it? If he got the press kit, he's seen my picture."

"Gérard proposed sending an e-mail message about an incident that only you and he witnessed."

"I can tell him what he said about Papa's accident. We were in Papa's car, just the two of us. I'd hate to dredge up memories of that experience. But he'd remember, and know that only I could report it."

"Telephone Gérard. Tell him the details. Trust him to transmit the essentials. When Grischevich recognizes you, we will send him an invitation to the show, and offer travel and hotel expenses. He is essential to the family reunion publicity."

Silently, I sip my tea and mull over how to tell Gérard the details of that conversation with Hampton. I don't doubt that Grischevich is Hampton, but I wonder if he'll remember what he said about Papa's death in exactly the way I do? Time changes the memory of events or what one chooses to remember. Hampton may not want to remember. He needed to get away and forget.

All the while I'm thinking, Jean-Louis is talking. He has an idea for a transgender Easter show. He's excited. The scene he imagines is so bizarre, I don't bother to listen. I've got more pressing problems to work out.

"I trust you like the Easter scenario, Violetta. I will speak to Christophe about it." He lifts my hand

and air-kisses it, leaves euros for our tea, and steps briskly out of the tearoom and across to the Métropole.

Waiting in line at the taxi stand, I have fantasies about meeting Hampton or Tomas Grischevich. I see him standing in front of the Métropole on a snowy afternoon, handsomely dressed like the Cossack dancers in the Bolshoi troupe I saw in Moscow. He's holding a long-stemmed red rose for me. The center doors of the Métropole open. I'm standing there, framed by the doors. He recognizes me at once, cries "Violetta" with a Russian accent, rushes to me, and we embrace.

A taxi drives up and takes the party waiting ahead of me. I'm next.

Another scene occurs to me. Hampton or Tomas looks seedy and down-and-out, like the Russian newcomers playing their accordions and panhandling in the Métro. Huddled in a dark backstage corner, he's come to see me, but he doesn't want to be seen. I recognize him, call his name, and he runs away.

Finally, a taxi comes to take me home to reality on rue Frochot. Before unlocking the door, I hear Leo purring. Inside, I find Hope's suitcases and a note from her on the kitchen table.

Dear Violet,
I'll come home after my shift at the restaurant—
around eleven tonight.
Love, Hope

Her note gives me a warm, mushy feeling like home-cooked oatmeal. Hope's coming to my place and she's calling it home. I go into the bedroom, light a candle on Josephine's altar, and stand there thinking about Hope's coming into my life, her linking me to Marie, the possibility of finding Hampton. And thanks to my faithful friend, Jean-Louis, I'm back onstage. I feel my pulse celebrating.

It's almost dark outside. The flicker of the little candle throws its light over the room. If I'd let my own inner light shine like that, I'm thinking, I could have lit up that uninspired rehearsal this afternoon. That's what Josephine would have done. I've got to carry her spirit, carry her light into the Métropole. Just now, though, I should call Gérard.

After an hour of busy signals, Gérard answers his phone. He asks me to dictate everything I can remember about the incident with Hampton. He wants more details, like what Hampton and I wore that day. He wants to know about things I can't remember: What route did we take on our drive from the train station? Were there any unusual sights? What was the weather like? The effort of relating a painful memory is draining. I need a nap after talking to Gérard. I strip down to my undies and fall into bed, out like a light.

A key unlocking my door disturbs my sleep. I sit up, ready for a showdown with a robber. Then I remember that Hope now has Sylvia's key to the apartment. I fall back onto my pillow and call, "Is that you, Hope?"

"It's me. Sorry to wake you up."

The candle has burned out. My room is dark. I turn on the bedside lamp and look at the clock. Ten forty-seven. "It's not late. Come on in and tell me about your evening."

"In a minute. I want get out of this dress." I hear her footsteps patter back and forth. She goes into the bathroom, closes the door, muffling the sounds of the toilet flushing, water running, brushing teeth.

The bathroom door opens. Ordinary sounds of human household companionship. Sounds I've needed to hear.

At my bedroom door in a terrycloth robe, Hope asks, "May I bring you a cup of hot chocolate or tea?"

I'm startled by the offer. Delighted and confused, I hardly know which to choose. At last I say, "Hot chocolate, please." I try to use an ordinary voice, so she won't know that I'm bowled over by her company and caring gesture. Then I wonder if I have chocolate in the cupboard. On second thought, I realize Hope must have bought some.

Soon the aroma of chocolate is in the air. Hope tiptoes in with a cup for me and a glass of sparkling water for herself. She sits on the edge of the bed. I move over, so she'll have more room.

"Make yourself comfortable," I tell her. She lifts her little rump and sits squarely on the bed, peering into her glass. I sip the hot chocolate, the best I've ever tasted. She looks sad. I wonder if she's sorry she's moved in. Is she unhappy about the show? Or is she missing André?

"What's got you down? Missing André?"

"It's not him. I called Faith today. She already knew about the mother-daughter act. Mom talked to her. She knows Mom is very upset."

"What does Faith think?"

"She said Mom was deeply hurt, that I ought to see a therapist about mother-daughter stuff, and that I need to repair my relationship with Mom. She babbled on about loyalty, my shifting allegiance to you, and how painful it's been for Mom. I got upset."

"What did you say?"

"I told her Mom feels disconnected from us both now. I asked her to come over with Mom and see the show. We could talk about family matters face-to-face here, if they come."

"You think they might come?"

"She said Stuart would love a trip to Paris. I told her to make the travel arrangements for Mom and Bill Knox, too. They should take the same flight, and make reservations at the same hotel. I gave her the dates of the show. Urged her to be here for the closing, the cast party, and all."

"What did she say?"

"She said she'll get back to me. She said it the way a dentist's receptionist says she'll phone you if there's a cancellation. It left me feeling sad and almost sorry I'd called."

"Be glad you called. Proud of yourself! One of you had to take the first step. And you and I have a deal, don't we? To make things better with our sisters. You spoke honestly to her and you invited her to come. Good!"

"Mom and Faith probably will come. And Stuart. And maybe Bill, too. I want them all, but especially Mom, to see how well you and I work together. I want to change her heart and mind. I want to talk with Mom and Faith and you about how to become a caring family."

"You think you can talk people into being a caring family?"

"In theater we do. We all help each other to make a show work. For the run of a show, theater people function like a family."

"That's the rare production with good theater people, baby. Marie and me, you and Faith—we're not acting. We're real relatives living real lives. Families have histories much longer than the life of a show. Families pass on hearsay and superstitions, grievances and insults, more stress on the bad stuff than the good, more regretting instead of rejoicing. I had to get away from that kind of family life. Maybe we can use what we learn in show biz to make a real life family work."

"Sometimes the real life family seems surreal," Hope says.

"Surreal? There you go again, stumping me with one those Spelman College words. I'll have to buy a giant dictionary with you around." Tapping the cup, I say, "And I'm buying this kind of chocolate. It's delicious. Is there any more?"

"Would you like more?"

"No, thanks. Have a cup yourself. It's soothing." Hope remains beside me for a while. I fall asleep trying to imagine how Hampton and Marie look now, but I can't picture them in my mind's eye.

21

Backstage at the Métropole, Monique and I are reading the bulletin board notices. "The rehearsal hours have been increased. I wonder why?" Monique says.

Sure enough, they've added another hour a day. As it is now, I'm close to collapsing at the end of rehearsals. One more hour will wipe me out. Can't admit it though. I stand near the board, leaning on my cane, listening to comments of others reading about the change.

"That's OK with me. Another hour of rehearsal, another hour's pay," says Odile.

"*Des heures supplémentaires? Pourquoi?*" Michel, one of the dancers, asks in his Haitian accent. Everyone who sees the schedule wants to know why an hour has been added. Finally, Pascal Roussel, always in a hurry, flutters by. Calling, "Pascal, Pascal," and pointing at the notice with my cane, I get his attention. "Pascal, why an additional rehearsal hour?"

"*O*pening night is for VIPs. Monsieur Breton's business associates, Suzanne's friends. The show must open with perfection," he says without slowing down.

Curious about advance sales, I chat with the stage door manager. He's also curious. He phones the box office and is told that opening night is sold out and sales are higher than usual for the rest of the show. We gossip about the new costume designs and plans for more dramatic lighting. "*C'est la publicité,*" he says, handing me a copy of *Parisnuit*, opened to a page with a picture of Hope and me. I scan the article next to the picture. It's disturbing. Suddenly, I'm worried sick. I've got to talk to Hope.

In the dressing room we share, I tell Hope, "The publicity about the show is stirring up a lot of interest, but it makes me nervous."

"Stirring up interest is good. Why are you nervous?" She stares at her mirror, plucking her eyebrows and searching for flaws in her flawless skin.

I tell her mirrored reflection, "It started out as a cozy holiday show for families. It's grown into a gospel spectacle for fat cats, a promotion piece to attract backing for the next show. They've hired a pricey costume designer who does music hall extravaganzas. They want to fire the kid doing the lighting, replace him with a lighting technician who does pyro effects. And the hype in the press about you and me just isn't true. Have you seen the latest *Parisnuit*?" I'm clutching the magazine, my hand shaking.

"What are they saying about us?" She looks away from the mirror and finds my face in full frown.

"They've made up a story about me abandoning you as a young child." I'll translate: 'Hope Fields was reared in poverty in a rural Kentucky foster home. Her childhood, like Josephine Baker's, was harsh and impoverished. She ran away to Atlanta, Georgia, where she was a street performer, like Josephine. Discovered by a dance teacher in Atlanta, she trained at the Atlanta Center for Dance Education where she studied before launching a search for her mother. Recently reunited, the renowned cabaret entertainer and music hall sensation Violet Fields and her daughter, Hope Fields, share with you their first Christmas together. Performing as a mother-daughter team for the first time, Violet Fields, a latter-day Josephine Baker, and Hope Fields, a future Josephine Baker, will bring you a program of

African American Christmas spirituals and gospels with background singers and dancers from their native Kentucky.' Doesn't this crap upset you?"

"The rest of the cast doesn't want to be considered background," Hope says. "Ignoring their nationalities and saying they are from Kentucky will upset them for sure. This isn't good for cast morale and the family spirit we've been building."

"What do you think of their lies about our relationship?"

"We started it with our make-believe spin. Public relations people added a layer to appeal to the public's stereotypes. When a black American woman appears on the stage or screen in France, comparisons are made with Josephine."

"May the French always remember Josephine! In the States, her memory has been neglected. She's been nearly forgotten. I'm honored by the comparison," I say.

"I'm not. I don't want to be called the future Josephine Baker," Hope says. "I want to be recognized for my unique style and talents. I want to be the future Hope—Hope Grayson or Hope Fields." She pauses and smiles about the names. "Anyway, I'm myself. I like the sound of Hope Fields. What I'm saying is that I want the freedom to be myself rather than be like somebody else."

I glance at the postcard image of Josephine photographed in a white gown and feathered headdress. "The day we were assigned this dressing room, I taped this Josephine Baker postcard on my mirror. I need the inspiration of her image. I understand you wanting to be your own person. But I wonder who has been a model for you?"

Looking thoughtful, Hope takes her time coming up with an answer. "I've never concentrated on one individual as a model. I like several vocalists. I see dancers with styles I admire. But I don't want to do what they do. I want to find my own modes of expression. I want to be original."

"That's powerful. That's smart." I'm quiet for a moment, thinking over my own life and work. I never aimed at being original. I wanted to earn a living, feel successful from time to time. I imitated the great vocalists and best dancers. I never expected to be great myself.

"You've got the right idea, Hope. You've got confidence, self-assurance, ambition. And you've got what it takes—star quality."

"Ten minutes. Ten minutes to rehearsal," Pascal's assistant announces over the speaker system.

Hope says, "When you were my age, you had models and heroes because you only saw their public selves. Now we get media stories about private lives and personal problems of public figures. It's hard to find a total persona you can admire today. So young people have to look inward and reach for their own personal best."

"It's a media thing. It's being done to us in this magazine," I moan and toss the copy of *Parisnuit* onto Hope's dressing table. "If the cast has seen that article, there could be some ugly moods in rehearsal today."

Hope is on her feet, deep breathing, bending, and stretching. Between breaths, she says softly, "Don't worry. I'll deal with the cast."

I leave her in the dressing room doing her warm-up routine. Go out, check the mood, and talk to them, jolly them up, I tell myself.

169

Walking is painful today. I'm leaning heavily on the cane. Only five dancers are onstage. They *bonjour* me, but in a reserved way. It's not the warm, hearty greeting I usually get. In a huddle, they're talking among themselves. I can tell what they're saying isn't good. I mosey over to my position, front stage right, next to the piano.

"Last call for rehearsal," Pascal's assistant booms. The rest of the cast saunters onstage grumbling remarks, the unsettling sounds of disgruntled workers ready to strike. I'm wishing Hope would come, so I'd have someone onstage to exchange glances with. No one even looks at me. What's keeping her? She knows the cast may be tense. She may not want to face them.

Then I hear the patter of her footsteps. In her white leotard and black tights, Hope runs in, stopping at center stage. She says with authority, "Before we start this rehearsal, I want to say a few words about an unfortunate article in the current issue of *Parisnuit*." She holds up the copy. "Violet brought this to my attention. There may be similar articles in other publications."

"Three others," somebody says.

Hope continues, "I know short-run variety shows like ours need creative publicity. However, I don't like the kind of material *Parisnuit* is running. What struck me as especially offensive was the reference to you, the cast, as background figures. You are wonderful, talented individuals with interesting, diverse histories and your own national traditions. You are essential to the production, not background figures. And none of you is from Kentucky!"

With a release of tension, laughter fills the stage.

"Lies, distortions, misrepresentations of who we are and what this show is trying to accomplish can undermine our rapport," Hope says. "The family spirit we've cultivated can be eroded if we let sensational rubbish influence how we view each other, how we work together." She's interrupted by a burst of applause. "Try to put it aside, ignore it. Concentrate on polishing the show in the short time that remains. Violet and I need your wholehearted support and goodwill. We know what each of you brings to the show. It won't work without everybody's unique contribution." Again they applaud. I'm clapping loudest, applauding her being honest and sincere, and clearing the air.

Using Pascal's usual command to begin the rehearsal, Hope says, "Start the music!" Pascal, standing beside me, heaves a sigh of relief and steps forward, arms gently swinging with the beat of the medley. Rehearsal is underway.

When Hope takes her place beside me, I reach for her hand, squeeze it, and let go with the release a tired runner feels on passing the baton to the next runner in the relay.

22

Whenever the telephone rings after midnight and before daylight, I prepare myself for bad news. I stir on the second or third ring, remembering that Hope is near the phone in the living room. Another ring, and I hear her groggy, "*Oui. Allô.* Hello?" After a pause, she says a few words quietly into the phone, and then calls me. "Violet, it's for you. A man calling you. Wake up. It's important."

I pick up the bedside phone. "Hello?"

"Hello, who is speaking?"

"Violet. Violet Fields."

"Madame Fields, this call is from Russia. I need confirmation. You are searching for a missing brother in Russia?" asks a deep voice in a strange accent.

"Yes, for Hampton Garfield." Instantly, I'm fully awake. "He was a US Army sergeant, captured in Korea in 1950 or '51."

"When was the last time you saw him?"

"At our father's funeral in Louisville, Kentucky."

"What did you call your father?"

"Papa."

"What did your father call your mother?"

"He called her Sugar Lump."

"Your brother brought a horse trainer home to meet you. The name of the trainer, please?"

"Pierre Prince." I'm getting impatient. His questions are like a blind man's fingers tracing the face of someone he once knew.

"Just one more question. Where was the piano in your family's house in Louisville?"

"There was no piano. I always wanted one. Saved my pennies, hoping to buy one."

In a familiar voice, the man says, "And I saved my pennies, hoping to buy a racehorse, Violetta Mae Garfield, alias Violet Fields." He hoots, and then it sounds like he's sobbing.

"Hampton? It's you, Hampton!" I'm laughing and crying as I speak his name.

Hope, standing at my bedside in her nightshirt, let's out a gleeful shriek. "It's Uncle Hampton!"

"Is that your daughter I hear?" he asks.

"She's Marie's daughter—and mine, too. I'll explain later." He wants to know about Marie. He remembers Billy Knox. I ask if he knew that Mama had died. He says he knew she would be gone by now. I tell him she died in '59—a stroke. He doesn't linger over her death.

He says he's happy that I'm still in show business and in Paris. I tell him about Stanley, and about being in Moscow once with Stanley. Hampton says he lives ninety kilometers from Moscow where he would not have heard a jazz band was visiting. I ask about his family. He speaks proudly of his children: two daughters and a son. Irina, a physician, who is married to a physician. They have two sons and live in Moscow. Natasha, a civil engineer in St. Petersburg, is divorced, no children. Anatoly, his son, is a forest manager in Siberia. Talking more slowly, sadly he tells me his wife, Svetlana, died last year. "But I have my horses," he adds, sounding cheerful again. "Twenty-two handsome Arabian thoroughbreds. I'm a breeder and co-owner of a farm. Our horses do well at international auctions."

"You go to auctions abroad? Do you ever get to France, to Paris?"

"I once had the chance to take horses to an auction in France, but Svetlana was having chemotherapy treatments. She was too weak to be on her own, so my partner went. I would like to visit Paris and to see you again. But wait, tell me, how did you find me?"

"Through horses. That was the main clue. When you were a kid, you loved horses."

"From time to time, I thought about searching for you. I thought about Marie, too."

"Well, what about coming to Paris to see your sisters? Marie's flying over in December to see Hope and me in a show." I'm getting excited. I pump it up. "Marie and Billy will be in Paris for the last performance. Marie's other daughter, Faith, and her husband may be here." Hope is nodding and smiling her encouragement. "You must come, Hampton. Bring your kids. It would be a great family occasion—a long overdue family reunion."

"I would like to see you and Marie."

"Did you get information about the show?"

"Somebody sent information about the show and flights to Paris. I wish I could get away, but this is the busy season. If I can find somebody to manage things here, I'll try to come. I can't promise, but I'll try."

"Bring your children. They ought to meet their cousins. And I want to meet my Russian nieces and my nephew. We've got a lot of catching up to do."

"All right, Violetta Mae. Still the bossy big sister. If I come I do not want any contact with American authorities. I trust you can understand my situation."

"Sure, I understand."

"By the way, thanks for bothering to find me. It could not have been easy."

"I'd like a mailing address and your phone number," I say rummaging for paper and pencil in the drawer of the night table.

"The best way to reach me is by e-mail," he says, sounding guarded.

"Now that I've found you, I've got to see you. Seeing you again would be the payoff for me," choking back tears. "If you can't bring your kids, bring their pictures."

With Hampton repeating that he'll try to come and me urging him to, we find words to end the call. I hang up.

In the still, chilly darkness of the November morning, Hope and I reach for each other's hands. I'm speechless after the conversation, over thousands of kilometers and a dozen national borders, linking me to a brother I haven't seen for more than half a century. Before I can talk to Hope, I have to play the conversation over in my head from beginning to end to fix in memory his tone of voice, his every word. He spoke slowly with pauses, like someone who doesn't use English much.

After a while, Hope says, "Do you think he'll come?"

"I don't know. He said it's his busy season, but he'll try to come."

"Imagine having cousins in Russia. Mom needs to know about them. We've got to tell her you've actually talked to Hampton."

I look at the illuminated hands of the clock and say, "It's too early and too late to call Louisville. Wait until afternoon."

"I can hardly wait. It's all so exciting. Did he get information about the show?"

"Yes, e-mails reached him, thanks to Gérard. We ought to get back to sleep. We need to be well rested for the rehearsal."

Hope tosses and turns on the sofa bed until the rhythm of her breathing tells me she's fast asleep. I'm awake for a long time thinking about Hampton. I wish I'd asked him to write. Seeing his handwriting would give me a sense of what he's like. I should have said, "If you can't come, send pictures of yourself and your children, your home and your horses."

He sounded vigorous. He's probably in good shape, being active around stables and outdoors, but I should have asked about his health. I wonder what he suffered in prison camp and afterward. How has he made a life for himself in Russia? Learned the language and customs? How did he meet his wife? How has being black—and Hampton is a very dark brown—affected how he's been accepted? Or rejected? Was he ever a Communist? Did he struggle with the question of whether or not to return to America? To Louisville? My head is spinning with questions. Is Hampton sorry that I've been guided to him? Is he sorry he called?

If Hampton comes, he'll want no part of the family reunion publicity Jean-Louis has in mind. I fall asleep finally, making a mental list of things Jean-Louis must not do or say if Hampton somehow gets here.

***

It's midmorning when the phone wakes me up again. Hope doesn't pick it up. Maybe she's in the bathroom. Or she's out. Two more rings. Almost rolling onto Leo, who springs off the bed, I turn over and take the call.

"Allo."

"Hello. Violetta Mae?"

"Marie?"

"Yes, phoning from Louisville. How are you?"

"I'm pretty well. I'm fine, just fine. Hope and I were going to call you in a few hours. You're up early. What time is it there?"

"I guess I beat you to it. Happy Thanksgiving." She sounds chipper. "It's four a.m. here. I'm up early, putting the turkey in the oven. We're having four couples for dinner. Twenty-five pound turkey, so I'm getting an early start. What are you and Hope doing for Thanksgiving?"

"It's not Thanksgiving in France. It's a regular weekday, a workday. I was going to call to tell you I've heard from Hampton. He telephoned from Russia a few hours ago."

"Hampton's alive? Praise the Lord! Let me sit down for this." I hear her dragging a chair. "He telephoned? How did he sound? What did he say?"

"He sounded older, of course, and cautious, almost suspicious. He's doing well—co-owns a horse farm, breeds Arabians. Twenty-two Arabian thoroughbreds," I say matter-of-factly. Given her acquaintance with horse racing, I know it will blow her mind.

"Wow! That's a big operation. And he's a co-owner? My goodness! Bill will find this news very interesting. I've got a notepad here. Let me jot this down. What else did he say?"

I repeat as much as I remember of our conversation. Then I tell her not to broadcast the news about Hampton all over Louisville. "He said flat-out he doesn't want any contact with American authorities. So what I've told you is confidential.

Don't mention him at Thanksgiving dinner. Don't even tell Billy Knox."

"But I trust Bill completely. We don't keep secrets from each other. Does Hope know about Hampton?"

"She knows."

"May I speak to her?"

"She's out. Maybe I shouldn't have told you he called." I'm silent for a while for the dramatic effect. "I hope you care enough about Hampton not to expose him or jeopardize his situation. OK, you can tell Billy that Hampton is alive and in Russia. That's enough for now." That old feeling, the need to be in charge and to control Marie, creeps up on me.

"Maybe we will go to Paris. If Hampton is there, and if we could meet his kids—that would be thrilling." Marie's voice leaps up an octave on "thrilling."

"You must tell me how you located him," she says. In a stern voice she adds, "You and I have a lot to talk about. We need to discuss the matter of you claiming that Hope is your daughter. Alienation of affection is what I think it is. My lawyer says I don't have grounds for a case. But I want you to know I resent your drawing her into your web like a black widow spider."

I'm sure Marie had practiced that line knowing it would hurt me; and it does. But I am not in the mood to take her on. Instead, I admit I've enjoyed pretending Hope's my daughter. Then I say, "You never knew I lost a baby, a son when he was an infant." I pause to let that news sink in. "I've needed to feel like a mother onstage for just a few weeks."

"No, I didn't know. Oh, I'm so sorry, Violetta. There's a lot I want to know about you. We need to make up for lost time. Ask Hope to call me, please. I need to talk to her."

"I'll tell her. I'm glad you called, Marie. Have a great Thanksgiving."

After we hang up, my heart has a meltdown. Within hours, I've talked to my long-lost brother and to Marie. It's almost too much to contain. Still in bed, I'm imagining Marie in her ultramodern kitchen roasting a huge turkey. I'm sure she's tortured by the thought of keeping the news of Hampton to herself. She'll spill it all at dinner, I know.

It's chilly. I pull the duvet under my chin to enjoy the warmth a little longer, and to think about Hampton. He was born with horses on his mind. As soon as he could walk, he was astride a mop or a broom galloping around the house. Later, he had an imaginary horse named Sammy. Walking along the street, he'd suddenly mount Sammy and trot ahead of me. On Saturday afternoons, I took him to cowboy movies. He didn't care about the cowboys' brawls and shootouts. He only watched the running of their horses. In school he drew pictures of horses in all his notebooks. Out of school, he could be found with two or three other boys at the track. They talked about staying small and boyish so they could be jockeys.

By the time Hampton was twelve, he had grown too tall to be a jockey. His ambitions had grown, too. About that time, Papa found jobs for him at the track. Hampton would come home in the evening with mud and horse muck all over his sneakers, and proud of it. He never showed any interest in baseball or football, and he wasn't wild about girls; but he sure was horse crazy.

Gérard must know a good deal about Hampton by now. I've never laid eyes on Gérard, don't even know his surname. I wonder what he's told Jean-

Louis about Hampton? If Hampton does show up, I don't want him in jeopardy. I hope I can trust Jean-Louis's judgment in this situation. I can trust Hope. She's discreet and she's smart. And I can trust Josephine. She's not going to tell anything to anyone—anyone but me.

At that moment above the altar in an oval of white light, Josephine appears.

"Come on down, Josephine. I've got a lot on my mind this morning. I need to see you." The sight of her is comforting. Her presence tells me everything's going to be all right.

She hums softly, then a little louder. I catch the tune: "Sonny Boy." Her voice fills the room like it's coming through big speakers. "When I'm old and gray, dear / Promise you won't stray, dear / I love you so, Sonny Boy." The song is a calming lullaby. Josephine says, "Violet, you've recovered your niece and located your brother. Embrace them. Hold them close." A breeze stirs the curtains, wafts over my bed, and she's gone.

I hear a key in the door; the door opens, and I feel a draft. "Hope, is that you?"

"I'm back from my jog. Only did half an hour. It's too cold and damp," she says coming into my room. "Hey, you're still in bed! Better get up if you want to be at rehearsal on time."

"I haven't been sleeping. Marie phoned with Thanksgiving greetings. She wants you to phone her."

"Did you tell her about Hampton's call?"

"I did and she was 'thrilled' to hear about him," I'm mimicking her voice.

"Thanksgiving? So it is. And you had a visitor, didn't you?"

"How do you know?"

"The smell. There's something in the air. Sorry I missed her." She smiles at me affectionately. Shifting to her bossy manner: "On your feet, Madame Fields. Get into some clothes. We've got a dress rehearsal and one more chance to polish our mother-daughter act."

23

Three days after the dress rehearsal, our show is opening. Locking my apartment door, I check to be sure I have everything I need in my tote bag: slippers, pills, publicity photos, pens for signing autographs, and the rabbit's foot on the key chain Stanley gave me for good luck. He'd rubbed nearly all the fur off by the time he gave it to me. I wish Stanley were here to tell me to be cool, that everything will be all right. And I wish Hope hadn't gone on an errand with André just before the opening.

I go downstairs one-step at a time, not wanting to risk stumbling or falling. At the bottom of the stairs, where chill and dampness have slipped indoors, I tie my brown fleece cape at the neck and pull on the hood.

Sylvia opens her door and says, "A limousine waiting for you. Your opening night and you wear that old cape. You look like a monk, not like a star. Anyway, break the legs!"

The driver, young and Maghreb looking, is courteous. Guiding me into the roomy back seat, he doesn't seem annoyed about waiting. He says he knows a fast route to the theater. In the icy drizzle, very few people are on the streets. It's a stay- at-home evening even if one has tickets for a show.

The lights on the Métropole's marquee are ablaze with "*Les Belles de Noël*—Violet & Hope Fields." Posters all over Paris announce the show. The box office reports a steady sale of tickets. Still I'm nervous about tonight—opening night—and the rest of the run.

At the stage door, the attendant looks up from his girlie magazine when I come in and slips it into the pocket of his overcoat. *"Bonsoir, Madame Fields. Vous arrivez de bonne heure,"* he says looking at his watch. I explain that Jean-Louis sent a car for me to be sure I'd arrive early. Besides, I like getting to the theater before the cast and musicians appear with their first-night hang-ups, superstitions, and jitters that make for tension.

In the dressing room, I turn on the lights and blow a kiss to the picture of Josephine. The wardrobe mistress has hung our costumes in the room. The rose taffeta dressing gown and apron I wear in the first act are comfortable. I wish I didn't have a costume change into that gold lamé cocktail dress.

I turn to the mirror and gaze at my face, more like a grandmother's than a mother's. Not waiting for the stylist, I begin covering wrinkles and moles with the liquid foundation makeup, brush back my short salt-and-pepper afro away from my face. More carefully than usual, I pencil my eyebrows so they resemble a matched pair, so one is not rounded and the other arched. "One eyebrow is Romanesque, the other Gothic," Hope told me yesterday.

The cast begins to stream in. My door is ajar so I can hear them, glimpse reflections in the mirror. I know their voices, know who's here. Greetings are scarce and hurried. Footsteps brisk—they canter or trot or skip. I feel the tension mounting. I take the rabbit's foot from my bag. Squeezing it, I close my eyes and whisper, "Sing with me tonight, Josephine." I begin to feel grounded.

Jean-Louis, crowing *bonsoirs* and *tout va biens* along the corridor, is backstage to reassure and romance the cast and stage crew. I'm sure he's kissing cheeks, patting *derrières*, doing whatever he thinks will enhance the energy of the performance. He doles out bottled water, aspirin, antacids, and decongestants; and promises post-performance treats.

At my door, he announces, "Violetta, a full house. Dozens waiting to buy standing room. You are still *une vedette.*"

"I'm hyped up enough. I don't need your pep talk," I insist. I reach out for the cup of coffee he offers. He sits on the chair at Hope's end of the dressing table. The mirror reflects his woebegone expression. Sipping the coffee, I look at him for a while before asking, "What's the matter, Jean-Louis? You were out there lifting everybody's spirits a moment ago, and now you're down in the dumps."

"I miss Boris tonight."

"Yes, Boris has been on my mind, too." It's true. I'm worried Hope's search for our surprise, another Russian wolfhound, has delayed her. Jean-Louis seems consoled by the notion that I think of Boris. On his feet again, he sighs, "*Alors.*" After admiring his black leather jacket, white wool pants, and patent leather dress slippers in the full length mirror at the end of the room, he leaves me wondering when Hope will show up.

A few minutes later, breathlessly she blows in. "Mission accomplished. No matter how the show goes, there'll be a happy ending for Jean-Louis. We have another Boris for him."

"Where is he?"

"André has him. He'll bring him backstage after the show. I've had enough of dogs today." Hanging up her coat, Hope pauses to inspect her costumes: a white nightgown and a silver lamé outfit. Stroking the silvered tutu, she looks pleased. In her chair, she lights a stick of incense, closes her eyes, and takes herself into a trance. With my maternal smile, I gaze at her. Already, I'm into my character.

The wardrobe mistress, Marina, knocks on the opened door and comes in, closing the door behind her. Through the pins clenched between her teeth, she mumbles, "*Bonsoir, Mesdames,*" addressing our costumes. I slip out of my brown velveteen pants and blouse, adjust my bra, and with some effort get up so Marina can help me into the gown. From a pocket, she takes a pair of large pearl earrings and clips them on my lobes. She ties the apron, pins it in two places, and steps back to note where adjustments are needed. Another pin at the cleavage of the empire bust line and "*Voila,* Madame Fields." Satisfied with how I look, Marina turns to the nightgown for Hope.

"*Cinq minutes, Madame Fields, Mademoiselle Fields.* Five minutes," the caller cries. The call light overhead is flashing. As I step to the door, I blow a kiss to Hope, who's being gowned, and say, "*Bonne chance.*" Still in her trance, she may not have heard me; anyhow, she doesn't reply. To the picture of Josephine, I blow another kiss.

I need almost five minutes to make my way to center stage where I'm seated, wrapping gifts at a table and listening to a radio broadcast. The set is an old-fashioned bourgeois living room. In the corner at stage right is a small, bare pine tree; at the end of the show, a huge, abundantly decorated Christmas tree fills the corner.

Careful not to stumble and fall over the boxes, wrapping paper, and ribbons beside the chair, I take my place just as the orchestra strikes up a medley of songs from the show. "*Rideau,*" the stage manager says, and the curtain rises. A few bars of the medley are piped as if through the radio. Then Monique's voice, in French, recites "A Visit from St. Nicolas." The poem ends. The house is silent, the audience very still. From stage left Hope tiptoes toward me, sweetly singing "*Il est né, le divin enfant...*" It's a well-known carol. Voices of children in the audience join Hope in singing the refrain. A burst of applause follows her number. Hope waits for the applause to wane, and then she asks her "*Maman*" to sing some holiday songs. She sits at my feet looking adoringly at me. I'm radiant, enjoying the moment.

An enormous screen above the stage brightens with scenes of snow falling on Paris streets and village cottages. I swing into "White Christmas." The musicians, only ten of them, have the polyphonics of a full orchestra. At first I'm not projecting well enough. From the pit, the conductor signals: louder, project more. I forgot that the acoustics aren't the same as in rehearsal. The sound is different when the house is full. I breathe deeper, getting the voice up and out. When we move into "Winter Wonderland," I get it right. I'm grooving. There's an interval of chimes and bells. We do "Jingle Bells" as a duet, Hope dancing around the table in a girlish way. I tell her it's getting late, time for bed, and I sing "Santa Claus Is Coming to Town."

Hope curls up and falls asleep on the sofa on stage right. Five male dancers in snug Santa Claus suits spring onstage from the left, leap and twirl and leap toward the sofa, dancing in Hope's dreams. Images of the dancing Santas are enlarged on the screen. With a *grand battement* they dance off stage right. Then softly, pianissimo, offstage soprano voices sing the theme from Humperdinck's Hansel and Gretel. The voices grow closer:

"When at night I go to sleep, fourteen angels watch do keep

Two my head are guarding, two my feet are guiding..."

The chorus of women, white robed with long angel wings, dances onstage surrounding the sofa where Hope sleeps. Among them, I see Josephine fleetingly. "Stay with me, Josephine," I whisper.

In a lively four-part version of "Angels We Have Heard on High," I sing with the chorus. Josephine is singing with us. I finish wrapping gifts, get up without straining, and walk over to the tree where I place the gifts, then stand looking down at Hope lovingly. I don't have to force the expression at all. The music ends. The audience applauds, cheers, and whistles.

The stage is gradually darkened. A scrim drops. "Silent Night," scored for flute and clarinet, is played in darkness. On the screen, a night sky is shown with a bright, pulsing star. When the lights come up the entire company, except Hope and me, is in front of the footlights. Women in red and the men in green sing "The Holly and the Ivy" and "O Christmas Tree," then go into a long dance number, smartly choreographed. The orchestra plays a medley of carols. From my angle behind the scrim, the dancers don't seem as surefooted as they were in the dress rehearsal. No matter. Act One is over. Whew!

Between the acts, I hurry—in my fashion—to the dressing room where Marina is waiting to help me with the costume change. I slip out of the rose taffeta and into a gold lamé gown with pearls crisscrossing my bosom. "Is this what mothers wear on Christmas morning?" Marina ignores my question at first. When I'm completely costumed, she says in her Slavic-French, "This is what a mother wears for a theatrical presence when Christmas morning is staged."

Act Two opens with solemn music as the company dances and sings "Follow That Star." Before three male dancers have been transformed into kings, their music starts. A minor glitch. They come on, quickening their pace, bearing gifts. The scrim lifts. The stage is brightly lit with the glory of Christmas morning. A beautifully decorated tree now occupies the corner.

As if waking up on the sofa, I stretch, yawn, and appear surprised to see the tree decorated with tinsel, Christmas balls, and lights. Hope is somewhere in the wings. The kings place their gifts under the tree, and then point to stage left where the dancers enter singing. Joined by a gospel choir of mature, robust singers, they rock the house with a jazzy arrangement of Handel's "Alléluia Chorus." Hope, shimmering in her silver costume, runs onstage to dance with the ensemble and sing "Go Tell It on the Mountain." The brass, tambourines, and gospel singers bring the hand-clapping audience to their feet. Still standing, they sing along with the refrain when I croon "Adeste Fideles." Beyond the footlights on the first row, Suzanne Dupont, Henri Breton, and some other corpulent cats are clapping and singing, too. I'm thinking this is the best I've ever sung. The audience raves. It feels grand.

The show ends with "Joy to the World," Hope's number. First she sings it straight, sings it gospel style with the choir, then dances with even more vigor and grace than she displayed in the audition. Her image, dancing on the screen above, doubles the effect. She's wonderful, powerful. The cast and choir are onstage singing behind her. Two of the kings accompany me to center stage. As the curtain falls, Hope and I embrace and rock with joy.

The audience erupts with a standing ovation. After several curtain calls and presentation of bouquets to Hope and me, the audience's rhythmic clapping invites an encore. Hope goes on alone and gives them another round of "Joy to the World." The applause is deafening. The audience continues to clap and cheer long after we're offstage. All the way to our dressing room, Hope and I are arm-in-arm, congratulating each other.

"You were phenomenal," she gushes.

"Baby, you're the one who put it over. That ovation, it was entirely for you. You're the best, Hope. The best." I search my soul for a hint of envy. None. I'm genuinely pleased the audience loved her. Pleased and very proud.

"Sensational! All of you were sensational," Jean-Louis booms up and down the corridor. Suzanne Dupont, comes in, kisses Hope and me, and says, "It is the best show in Paris. I am very proud." She reminds us of the party she's hosting tonight for the cast, musicians, and crew. "I'll see you later at Maxim's," she says, then adds, "Take your time getting there, Violet." She's noticed I'm bushed. At the same time, I'm overjoyed about the response to the show.

Monique comes in, genuflects before me, and says, "Thank you for the chance to be in this show."

Odile, a step behind her, imitates the gesture and in a lighter mood, says, "You were the perfect mother." Others in the cast stop in to share their enthusiasm about the performance.

Over the chatter I hear barking, whimpering, and the padding of paws. Hope, already out of her costume and in a black sheath, says, "André's here with the dog. Where is Jean-Louis?" She opens the door.

"Congratulations. The show was superb," André says. He brushes Hope's lips with a quick kiss. A sleek Russian wolfhound pulls André away from her and toward me.

"It's the new Boris. Will someone find Jean-Louis?" I say. Nosy and fidgety, this Boris is sniffing everything. Hope leaves the dressing room to page Jean-Louis.

"I hope Jean-Louis is ready for another dog," I say to André, who's gripping the leash.

"Too late. We can't return him. The former owner is moving to Prague. And I can hardly wait to hand him over." André shifts his attention from the dog, and says, "Madame Violet, you can still bring down the house. Or more aptly, bring the house to its feet. You gave a great performance."

Moved by his compliment, I'm blinking back a tear when Hope returns with Jean-Louis. "It's a present from us," she tells him. New Boris sniffs Jean-Louis's patent leather slippers and trousers. He allows Jean-Louis to stroke his coat, lift his head, and look into his eyes. Suddenly, the dog is calmer.

"*Un coup de foudre!*" Jean- Louis announces and prances out with the dog on a leash.

I'm pleased to see my old friend in love again. "Move along now. I've got to undress and dress. Off you go to Maxim's. You deserve a celebration."

"What are you going to do?" Hope asks.

"I'm sitting here until Marina gets me out of this garb. Then I'm getting into my own clothes, and a limo is taking me home."

On leaving, Hope says, "Several critics came. I can't wait to see the reviews."

"Don't read the reviews," I tell her. "I never look at them until a show's ended. Reviews warp your artistry, mess up your mind about the work. Read them after the show closes."

As the rest of the cast is leaving, I call out as they pass: "Great dancing." "Thanks for good backup." "Have a good time." "Drink *une coupe*

190

for me." It's quiet backstage. Marina finds me half asleep. Resting my head on my arms folded on the dressing table, I'd drifted off.

I'm the last to leave the theater. The driver is waiting. He tells me there was a crowd at the stage door. They wanted me to autograph their programs. I'm sorry I missed them. It gives me a rush to sign my name for fans. But I didn't have the energy to hurry out; and fans don't like to wait. Anyhow, I'm eager to get home, light a candle at the altar, thank Josephine, and go to bed. The prospect of seven more performances is exhausting.

24

"They're here!" Hope cries from the living room.

"Who's here?" I call from the bed, not opening my eyes.

"Mom and Bill, Faith and Stuart."

"Here?" Startled, I sit bolt upright. The late-morning light frames the closed draperies. The clock shows eleven forty.

"Mom just phoned from their hotel. I said we'd meet them there in an hour. So get up and get a move on."

I've been preparing for two productions: *Les Belles de Noël* and a family drama without a title or a script. When I wasn't thinking about the numbers we sing, I was rehearsing lines for scenes with Marie and Billy Knox, Faith and her husband, and maybe Hampton, too. I'm worried about spending time with Marie. What do we have to talk about? How will she react when she sees Hope as my stage daughter?

Hope said Faith and Stuart will go back to the States a few days after the show; but Marie and Billy have a three-week excursion package. The notion of Marie in Paris for three weeks has had me leafing through guidebooks for places outside Paris for her to visit.

"Are you sure they want to see us right away? They must have jet lag. Don't they need to sleep?" I ask Hope.

"They want to see us now, and I want to see them. Come on, Violet, get up and get dressed. I'll help you as soon as I'm ready."

"*Alors, le jour de gloire est arrivé,*" I sing out.

Leaning on my cane in front of the open armoire, I can't decide what to wear. Hope comes in and reaches for the gray designer dress I haven't worn since the audition. It's the right choice. I should look my best for kinfolk who haven't seen me for a while.

In half the time it takes me alone, Hope has me dressed, downstairs, and outdoors. It's chilly, but the sky is clear. The taxi Hope's called pulls up. She tells the driver to take us to the Madison Hotel on boulevard Saint-Germain.

In the taxi, I murmur, "I'm glad they've arrived on a nice day."

"We're supposed to have good weather for the next two or three days," Hope says. "Good weather for sightseeing."

"And for our last performances. Last night's was better than the night before, don't you think?" I ask.

"I still think opening night was the strongest."

"You were terrific on opening night," I tell her. "The ovation was especially for you. The rest of us, including me, weren't at our best. I had trouble projecting. And nearly everybody had first-night jitters because friends and relatives were there. André and his mother were in the audience. Didn't that make you nervous?"

"I would have been, if I'd known they were there. I was expecting André to come only after the show—to deliver New Boris to Jean-Louis. The high point of the week for Jean-Louis was getting New Boris."

"Jean-Louis calls him Boris Nouveau," I remind Hope.

"Yesterday he named him Vladimir in honor of the Russian president."

The taxi turns onto boulevard Saint-Germain. I start perspiring and breathing heavily. Hope takes off her gloves, presses my gloved hands between hers, and whispers, "Be glad you're going to see her again. You took the first step—writing to her. And you and I have a deal, don't we?"

By the time we reach the Madison, I'm more relaxed. The receptionist, a jaunty middle-aged man, greets us. "*Bonjour, Mesdames.* Your party is waiting for you on the banquette at end of the lobby." The connection is evident, given our family resemblance. They spot us and wave.

The distance from reception to the back of the lobby is almost as long as the stage of the Métropole is wide. I'm holding Hope's arm as we approach at a slow pace. Faith and Stuart meet us midway. I pause to catch my breath. Faith and I brush cheeks. Hope and Faith kiss, laugh nervously, and walk ahead arm-in-arm. Stuart replaces Hope on my right. He's clean-shaven, dark-haired, slim, and taller than average. He flashes a boyish smile. I think I'm going to like him.

I'm reassured by his firm grip and small talk: "I've been looking forward to meeting you." "We saw a huge poster advertising your show." "Six more paces and you're there."

Marie has her arms around Hope, holding her close. Hope returns the embrace. I see that my stage daughter knows her true mother.

After fifteen years of separation, I'm standing before Marie. Stuart drops my arm. I rest both hands on my cane to steady myself. Marie steps closer, reaches out, clutches the sleeves of my quilted coat. I'm trembling, and she has tears in her eyes.

"Violetta Mae, I thought this day would never come." She hugs me. My arms feel weak as I hold her close.

Billy Knox shakes my hand and says, "Have a seat, Violetta Mae." Hope and Faith look on, taking in our meeting. Hope looks theatrical in her black cape; Faith casual in a tan turtleneck sweater and brown slacks. Unmistakably sisters, they would be mistaken for twins if their hairstyles were similar. The same height, their skin the same glistening copper. But Hope's close-cropped hair and pearl earrings dangling to her shoulders make her glamorous, more striking than Faith, whose hair is brushed back and twisted in a bun; only her diamond stud earrings sparkle. Each is lovely in her way. It's a relief that they're clearly happy to see each other.

Billy and Stuart stand beside us like gentlemen-in-waiting, in the upscale American male uniform: navy blazers, gray trousers, and loafers with tassels. Billy in a white shirt and a tie, dark blue with a pattern of horses. If I didn't know it was Billy, I'd need to be introduced. He's changed a good deal since I saw him at Lloyd's funeral, looking much older and more distinguished than before. It's his mustache and gray hair. Shoulders back, chest up, a military bearing, he's almost handsome.

I notice Marie is still trim in places where I've grown pudgy. Not a gray strand in her hair—a good dye job. She always looked like Mama—especially her mouth, its prim expression. She's dressed to the nines in an expensive beige suit, a neat, serviceable outfit for travel, accentuated by the mink jacket. Then I notice what look like emerald earrings. I wonder if they're real. Her anxious hands—hands satin smooth, nails manicured—flutter in her lap, calling attention to a diamond surrounded by emeralds on the ring finger of her left hand. I nod my verdict: they're real. Billy Knox has done well by my sister.

I wish Mama could see us now. The Garfield sisters in Paris, and nicely turned out. Marie married to a man who's a good provider. Mama would be satisfied that her prayers for Marie were answered, and that I'm more respectable than she'd expected.

"You look great, Marie. And you, too, Billy," I say looking him up and down.

"You're the only one left who still calls him Billy," Marie titters.

"And you're the only one who calls me Violetta Mae. I'm Violet now." Hearing my childhood name snatches me back to a time when I was miserable and scared. I want to be known as Violet.

"Oh, I don't mind if someone remembers me as Billy. It makes me feel young again," he says.

"You ordered champagne?" a waiter asks Stuart. On the tray are a bottle of Louis Roederer and six glasses. Stuart nods and takes the check. The waiter uncorks a champagne so pricey I've had it only at weddings and wakes. Holding high our glasses, we try to follow Billy's long, rambling toast that takes off in Knoxville, touches down in Cleveland, buzzes Los Angeles and Santa Fe, circles Moscow, and lands in Paris, with family names mentioned in every city. Afterwards Marie says, "Let's just drink to us. And to Hampton."

Before the bubbles dance up my nose, Marie has my ear. "How in the world did you find Hampton? I tried for years with no luck."

"Through a friend of a friend who has connections. I don't mean to sound mysterious, but how he tracks people is a mystery to me. Horses were key to finding him."

"You think he'll actually get here?" Billy asks.

"He said he'll try," I tell him.

"How long is a flight from Moscow to Paris, or do you think he'd come by train?" Stuart wonders.

Billy estimates the flying time and confuses matters by talking about various air routes and types of Russian planes. Stuart asks questions now and then, which encourage Billy to speak longer and louder about transportation in Europe and Asia, much of which he admits he's learned from the Internet in preparation for this trip. Marie and I, spared the discomfort of making conversation, pretend to listen. Standing apart, Hope and Faith appear to be having a lively talk.

Faith then comes and sits next to me. She tells me Hope is happier than ever. Taking my hand, Faith says, "I've wanted Hope to find herself, and I've wanted to find you."

Billy suggests we go up to their suite for a real drink. He's brought a rare Kentucky bourbon that he swears will make me homesick for Louisville.

Faith says, "I'd rather have something to eat." Stuart agrees.

"It's time for lunch anyway. Let's go to Le Petit Zinc. It's a short walk from here. It's a favorite of restaurant critics," Hope says.

"You kids should go to lunch. Bill and I want some time with Violet. We're going up to our room," Marie says and leads the way to the elevator. She looks proud and confident, the kind of self-confidence that gems, fur, and financial security give a woman.

Billy takes my arm and crosses the lobby with me. Faith and Stuart put on matching brown leather jackets and follow Hope, who calls out from the entrance, "I'll see you at the theater, Violet."

Marie, Billy, and I take the elevator to the top floor, where a hallway window frames the Eiffel Tower and Invalides amid Paris rooftops. Inside their suite, furnished in soft blues, caramel, and cream, Marie offers me a commodious chair. Before I've settled into the seat, she says, "It looks like you and Hope have become very close."

A well-rehearsed opening line, I'm thinking. I say, "She's a lovely young woman—and very helpful. I'm happy with her staying with me." I could have said happier and safer now that she shares my life, but I don't want Marie asking what it was like before.

Pouring three glasses of bourbon straight up, Billy says, "You've been a great help to Hope. We're grateful for all you've done." We touch glasses and say, "Cheers." I look from Marie to Billy and back to Marie, wondering who will follow his remarks with more to say, beginning with the word "but."

Billy continues, "But it's difficult for her to get started in the theater and music business in a foreign country. You know better than us how hard it is."

Marie says, "I don't want her to settle outside America. She'll lose touch with us. If she's really talented, she can make a name for herself back home. She could get into television commercials. Louisville has a new repertory theater where she can get a start."

"A new white repertory theater? Where she might get a part every three years?" I snap back.

"How can you say that? You don't know present-day Louisville." Marie sighs and shakes her head.

"I know what's happening in theater in the States. It's tough enough for us blacks in New York. Trying to work in Louisville would kill her spirit."

"I suppose you want her to stay here and be like a daughter to you. You want her to leave me, the same way you left Mama," Marie hisses.

"Order! Will the Garfield girls come to order? We didn't fly all the way over here for you to fuss with each other. We're here for a reunion—your Paris reunion."

"That's right. I don't want to quarrel. Bill and I want to see Paris and spend some time with Hope and with you."

"And maybe Hampton will show up," Billy says. "Saw him last when he was just a kid hanging out at the track, but I didn't know him actually."

"I've been telling Bill about Hampton. Remember that rocking horse he made for me? He told me to 'rock it fast like a jockey,'" Marie says, sips a little more bourbon, and smiles. "At school, when kids picked on me, Hampton always turned up to defend his 'baby sister.' And he was good with Mama, able to change her mood with a joke, that is, before Papa's accident. After that, something went terribly wrong between them." Marie stares into her empty tumbler. She knows what went wrong between Mama and Hampton, but she's not talking about it now. I don't want to speak of it either.

Billy, pouring for himself again, says, "You don't need another shot, darling. But what about you, Violetta Mae—I mean to say, Violet? Looks like you've hardly touched yours."

"I shouldn't be drinking at all. I'm diabetic."

"Me, too. And Mama was diabetic. I guess it runs in the family," Marie says sadly.

"I admit I haven't been careful enough about what I eat and drink."

"Hope's worried about your health. Do you have a good doctor?" Marie asks.

"A great doctor. But what can doctors do once you've got so much sugar in your blood?" I say.

"Like show business in your blood—and in Hope's," Billy says.

"I guess that's my cue. I should get going."

"Do you have to leave this early?" Marie says, glancing at her classy watch. "There's so much I want to know about you and Stanley."

"We'll have time for all that after the show ends. You're coming tomorrow night. Tickets for you— comps—are at the box office. You'll meet the cast at the party after the show and hear what they have to say about Hope's fabulous talent."

***

A taxi takes me back to rue Frochot. I need to rest—no, recover—before tonight's performance. On the steps, I stop to catch my breath. I hear my phone and Leo's meow, loud and insistent. By the time I unlock the door and get in, the ringing has stopped. Relaxed, comfortable again in my red kimono, I pick up the phone to hear the messages. Only one, from Gérard: "Good news. Your brother will arrive tomorrow at 16:50 at Charles de Gaulle Airport. A driver will bring him to the Métropole."

My heart does a cartwheel. Hampton is actually coming

25

Restless, Leo scampers about, jumping on and off my bed, not letting me nap. He's upset about something, maybe his bout yesterday with Vladimir. When Leo dashed to his perch in the kitchen, Vladimir, barking fiercely, followed him. "Well, Leo, Boris didn't bark at you, but he has passed on. Your world's going to be a little different now. So get used to it." He looks as if he understands.

Restless, I roll on my side, twist, turn, adjust, and readjust positions. To fall asleep, I'm using all my gimmicks—eye mask, easy listening music, deep breathing exercises. Nothing works. So I might as well get up and get ready for tonight. It's a big night—this closing. It's important for Hope to strut her stuff so Marie and Faith see her star quality. Jean-Louis has a lot riding on the show with potential backers coming. And me—I probably won't know until curtain time if Hampton makes it to the theater. Then what? If I talk to him before going on, I'll be too rattled for the performance. And if he isn't there, I'll be rattled, too.

I wish Stanley were here. I wanted him to know Hampton. Stanley would meet his plane, be there to welcome him, make sure he got to the show. I suppose I could ask Marie and Billy to meet him; but Charles de Gaulle Airport is confusing. They'd get lost.

Sitting on the bed, rubbing my swollen knee, I remember sitting on our Louisville porch with Hampton, bare feet dangling. It was the end of a hot August day, a day of endless chores. He was eleven; me, twelve. Marie, upstairs sleeping. "When I grow up, I'm going to be a movie star living somewhere far from Louisville," I told him.

"When I grow up, I'm coming back to Louisville once a year for Derby Day with my horses. I'll be living far from Louisville, too, farther away than you." Hampton must have had a sixth sense about his future.

Standing before the altar in my bedroom, looking at her photograph in top hat, white tie, and tails, I whisper, "Josephine, come along with me tonight. I want you there, pushing me forward, lifting me higher. I need your spirit."

In a burst of blue light like the flashbulbs of a dozen cameras, Josephine appears. She's smiling. Her perfume fills the room. She says, "Violet, you're on the eve of victory. Your family will see what Paris has given you and what you give to Paris. It's a gift— your gift to them. Their excitement about your work will be your reward."

"You've brought me here, Josephine. Seen me this far and shown me the way."

"Go honestly, directly into the events ahead. No detours, no short-cuts, no evasions. Live every moment deeply now. Live it and live it up! Don't worry, Violet. I'm with you." Her aura, the blue light that surrounds her, begins to fade. The aroma drifts away, and she's gone.

I feel new energy, almost youthful vitality. Singing the show's music, I go about preparing for the evening. The last show has to be the best. I'm in the mood to wow them all, especially my family.

A knock at the door and I know Jean-Louis and Vladimir are here. Ready to leave, I open the door.

"You look somber, Violetta. Are you going well?" Jean-Louis says as he leads me down the steps.

"I wish we weren't closing. A show like this ought to have a longer run."

"It is not the end. It is a beginning. Before you have wiped off the makeup and turned in the costumes, you will be thinking of the Easter show."

"Easter is months away. Tonight is what I'm wrestling with. It's going to be the longest and the shortest night of the year."

"The solstice, yes, the longest night. But how is it the shortest?" He pauses to search the sky before getting into the car. The evening air is chilly; there's a brisk breeze. Christmas lights amid the neon sex signs strike me as strange. But that's my Paris—sacred and profane.

"I just know time's going to fly by. The show will be over before I'm warmed up. And with my family all there. Gérard called. Did he tell you Hampton's coming?"

"I know. I've sent Gérard to meet him. He will escort your brother to the theater."

"Jean-Louis, you think of everything."

"Not quite. I forgot to reserve the restaurant near the Métropole for the cast party tonight. So it is at Fouquet's. It's just a few of the cast and your family. The choir is leaving for London; and the musicians have late-night gigs. It will be small, intimate."

"A good choice. Marie will adore being on the Champs Élysées at Fouquet's when she hears celebrities dine there. Tomorrow the party is on me—at my place. Hope and I are making lunch—that is, getting lunch—for the family. I want you to come. But don't talk to them about a family story for the press. I don't want that kind of publicity."

"You may regret it. But you've regretted other things I've done for you."

"I'm glad you had my apartment fixed up. I couldn't have invited them if it looked the way it used to. I don't know how to thank you."

"Oh, but you do; that is to say, you have. You have given me a new companion," he says, stroking Vladimir, "and a reprise in the business."

***

At the theater, Hope is already in the dressing room. Bursting with excitement, she says, "Uncle Hampton's plane has arrived! Gérard just called from the airport. I'm going to phone Mom. She'll be so happy." She takes her cell phone to the stage door where reception is good. When she returns, I ask, "What did Marie say?"

"She said 'That's thrilling news.' She's anxious to see him."

I can hear her voice rise on "thrilling." Wondering if Hampton will be drawn to Marie, I feel a pang of what Hope says is "sibling rivalry" and try to dismiss it. Getting on with the show is what matters; but it's hard to concentrate knowing Hampton will be here soon.

Monique, Odile, and others in the cast stop by the dressing room to tell Hope and me that they, too, are excited about this performance because our relatives will be in the audience. Jean-Louis, I'm sure, has aired his ideas about a family story among the cast. More now than before, the presence of family, the arrival of Hampton, and our reunion—all seem private and personal. I don't want to read about Hope, Marie, and me in a tabloid.

Marina comes in to help me into my costume. The taffeta gown easily slips over my hips. She remarks, "It is loose. You are now a size smaller." She pinches the fabric at my waist and holds it with pins.

"I haven't had time for lunch all week; and after the show I'm too tired to have dinner."

"We must take care of ourselves, Madame. We are no longer young." It is then that I look closely at her—her hair dyed russet, white at her scalp; liver spots on her hands; wrinkles in her neck. She told me she was born in Bulgaria, but she didn't say when. No time to ask. Marina moves on to another dressing room.

***

I'm onstage a few minutes before curtain time. Hope runs to me and says, "Hampton is in the audience, seated on the aisle two rows behind Mom and Bill. Come, you can see him."

From my center stage seat, I get up, step around the props—boxes and ribbons—and creep to the curtain. Hope pulls the curtain aside slightly and points. The house lights are up. I think I see him—dark complexion, white hair, sideburns, and mustache.

"Do you see him? It must be Uncle Hampton. That's the seat reserved for him."

"Yes, it must be Hampton." Still I'm not sure. My distance vision isn't what it used to be. "He looks older than Hampton should look," I tell her as she steers me back to my position. The curtains open, followed by an outburst of applause. I look beyond the footlights across the darkened theater in his direction and whisper, "Hampton, this show is dedicated to you."

The orchestra swings into the overture with brighter brass and more tremolo on the drums than in the previous shows. When Hope, softly singing *"Il est né, le divin enfant..."*, tiptoes onstage, the audience again applauds. Word is out. She's the star. I'm glad Marie's here to witness the excitement about Hope's appearance.

A blast of energy seems to lift the performance off the stage. The sequence of numbers, volume of music, combinations of instruments, quality of voices, vibrations of the gospel chorus, grace of the dancers, pace of the show—everything is in beautiful harmony. I sing a rousing "Angels We Have Heard on High," and rock back and forth with the chorus.

During intermission, everybody is energized. The cast is ready to celebrate. We have to rein in our enthusiasm before going on again, so as not to send it over the top.

In the second act, the dance to the medley is executed with brilliant precision. Then the three kings come onstage. When I join in the chorus, I hear in my singing the voice of Josephine—the voice of her later years. The gospel choir gives me the lead in the "Alléluia Chorus," and I carry it heavenward. The audience is swinging and swaying. My "Adeste Fideles" is even stronger than it was on opening night. I feel the spirit, the spirit of Josephine boosting my performance. Then Hope's "Joy to the World" brings down the house. At the end, everybody onstage is dancing. I'm dancing with them. Some people in the audience are dancing in the aisles.

After the fifth curtain call, the director, conductor, and choral director are invited to take a bow. The rhythmic applause and stamping of feet sound amplified. Another curtain call, and Christophe Michelet of the Métropole staff along with Suzanne Dupont and Jean-Louis come out and bow. Bouquets of flowers are presented, and roses are tossed over the footlights. The house lights are brought up, allowing us to see the audience. I look for Hampton and find him in the aisle surrounded by Marie, Billy, Faith, and Stuart. Marie's arm is around Hampton's waist.

In the center of the dress circle are André and his mother; Legrand, Midi, and Petit with their wives; Dr. and Madame Chang; Nurse Swindon; my neighbor, Sylvia the fortune-teller; and Claudine Roulin, who played for our audition. Another curtain call. "Enough!" I shout, eager to go backstage and get ready to be with Hampton. The curtains close. My right leg cramping, I limp offstage.

I'm still in costume when the family group comes crowding into the dressing room. I step back to give them room and give myself a view of Hampton before embracing him. The Army didn't stretch him any; he's about the same height, with the same stocky build he had in his teens. His hair—Hampton is the one who got what Mama called "good hair," unlike Marie and me—his hair is white, brushed back with neatly trimmed sideburns curving toward a full mustache—a thin goatee. Gray stands in his thick eyebrows. Narrow eyes, puffiness under them. He's darker than I'd remembered, now coffee-bean brown. A serious expression, forehead creased with frown lines. His face looks like it hasn't smiled often, hasn't found much to be happy about. His lips are quivering as if forming words for this moment—for me.

"Come here, Hampton, let me hold you." Without a word, he steps forward into my outstretched arms. We hug and hold on to each other. His body is tense at first, and then I feel him loosen up. I know I'm sobbing and he is, too, before I hear a joyful rumble in his chest and feel the ripple of his laughter and my own.

"Violetta Mae Garfield, my big sister, first friend, and playmate; and now you are Violet Fields, Paris's prima donna. And looking grand."

I want to tell him he looks good, but it's not true. He looks tired and worn, older than his years. "Hampton, I'm so happy you're here, so happy to see you again," I say. Everything else I've thought of saying on seeing him has evaporated from my mind like perfume from an open vial. I'm relieved when Marie takes things in hand and says, "I understand a car is waiting to take us to a restaurant where we can talk." Jean-Louis appears and says, "That is correct. We must leave now. The chauffeur will return for the others." With a tour guide's sweep of his arm, he has the group follow him to the car.

Hampton remains and says, "I am in Paris only through the weekend. Will we have some quiet time together?"

"This may be it. We've got a lot of catching up to do. Sit down." I point to Hope's chair, take my seat, and nod toward the door, signaling Hope, Odile, and Monique to leave.

"I have been missing from your life for a long time—more than fifty years. When I left Korea, my past was erased. I never thought I would see you again." He leans toward me, our knees almost touching, looking into my eyes as if he'll see something of Louisville in them.

"What happened to you in Korea? Your letters from the prison camp didn't say much. I got them—still have them somewhere. But there was never a return address, so I didn't know where to write you. Then the letters stopped."

Speaking slowly, thoughtfully, he says, "I can't recall what I wrote in those letters. I knew mail would be read and censored. I was never sure they would be sent." He pauses. "In the letters I could not mention locations. I was in the Twenty-fourth

Infantry Regiment of the Twenty-fifth Division, Eighth Army," he says in a rapid military way. "You see, although Truman ordered the armed forces desegregated, the Twenty-fourth Regiment was still all black. I served under a black officer, Lieutenant Leon Aaron Gilbert, a seasoned soldier, World War II veteran who had reenlisted. A dozen of us owe our lives to him."

"He saved your life—how?"

"We were in hilly country near Sangju under intense enemy fire for at least ten days. Men were tired and sick with dysentery. A white commanding officer ordered Lieutenant Gilbert to assemble us and charge an enemy outpost. Knowing it would have been a suicide mission, Gilbert refused. He said we would be killed. He was arrested and court-martialed. We heard he was sentenced to life in prison. Gossip about the incident circulated throughout troops in Korea. The abuse we took from white soldiers after that was terrible, worse than the enemy's assault. They called us Gilbert's yellow-bellied niggers."

"How awful for your morale."

"Morale was terribly low. To test our courage, another commanding officer—white—ordered our unit to repel an enemy attack. The entire unit was ambushed. Some of us were captured, sent to North Korea to prison camp. At first, we were held with white soldiers and treated badly—all of us. Most of us were sick, and we were always hungry—near starvation. I lost forty pounds. And was it cold!" He shivers and, with his hands at his mouth, breathes into his palms as if to warm them.

I'm thinking about how he endured those conditions and say, "But you survived. You're a survivor, Hampton."

"What may have saved us was that somebody ordered the racial segregation of prisoners. A good move for us Negroes. We got better treatment—less torture and some food. And we got some attention and respect from what they called reeducation teams. They had us in study groups on communism, comparing it to capitalism. They made us think about what we were going to return to in the States.

"When the truce was announced in September '53, we were told we had some choices—the chance to study a language, learn a trade, travel in China or the Soviet Union. The offers sounded good, better than any I would get in Louisville. So I refused repatriation, along with some others. Most went to China. A few of us went to Soviet Russia."

He sits back, folds his arms, like he's prepared to defend his choice. I don't need or want him to defend it. It was the right choice for him. I could relate to his wanting to be anywhere but in Louisville.

"But they said you were missing in action."

"Later I learned if you refused repatriation, you were declared missing. Army Intelligence and the CIA knew we were not MIA. They knew where we were, kept tabs on us for years."

"So you weren't alone?"

"There were others. But what matters now is that I am here. You cared enough to find me, bring me here. I had no idea I meant so much to you—that you would trouble yourself to look for me." He reaches for my hand, squeezes it, holds it.

"All these years, I've thought about you, wondered what had happened to you when it was said you were missing."

"You can understand why I didn't want to go back to Louisville." He shakes his head. "I could not go back with the guilt I felt. I couldn't face more of Mama's anger."

"You weren't responsible for Papa's accident, yet Mama blamed you. I told her it wasn't your fault. But she had to blame somebody. I've felt guilty about not staying there to work things out. Maybe I could have turned Mama around, persuaded her not to hold it against you. Anyhow, I'm glad you didn't go back."

Now holding both my hands in his, he says, "Getting out of Louisville did not relieve the guilt. When people ask about my family, I cannot tell the whole story. Could not tell Svetlana until many years after we were married. What happened that day at the track is something I relive every day." He drops my hands and goes into a hip pocket for a handkerchief. Wiping away a trickle of tears, he says, "I am very careful with horses, very disciplined. I want my son, Anatoly, to join me in managing the farm. But I would not want an accident to leave one of us dead, the survivor haunted by the memory of it."

He sighs, drops his shoulders, strokes his goatee a few times before saying, "You know how much I loved Papa, admired him. My carelessness was a factor. But the horse killed him. I tried to explain that to Mama, but she wouldn't hear it. I begged her forgiveness—hoped her Christian faith would allow her to forgive me. All these years, I have been in a prison of guilt and shame. She locked me in a prison in my mind where I am serving a life sentence."

A knock at the door. Jean-Louis says, "Monsieur, we are waiting for you." Hampton kisses my cheeks before leaving and says, "Violetta Mae, I have felt you and Marie might also blame me. I see now that you do not. I am profoundly grateful."

Profoundly grateful is what I'm feeling—and profoundly sad—saddened by our long silences, long absences, and misunderstandings.

***

Hope returns to the dressing room humming "Joy to the World." She dresses quickly. Odile and Monique, in their coats, join us. Odile helps me out of my costume, while Monique collects my personal items and puts them in my tote bag.

"Take down the picture of Josephine, Monique. She goes everywhere with me."

I need to rest a moment before getting dressed, but Odile won't let me. *"Dépêche-toi,"* Odile says over and over, hurriedly helping me into my brown velveteen suit and my cape. She ushers me to the car with such haste that I forget my cane. Hope, bringing it, says, "If you leave your cane behind, you must not need it."

Monique, with her tote bag and mine, follows us to the car. Waving to the cluster of people at the stage door, we apologize—*"Désolée"*—for our rushing away.

I look up at the marquee, now dark but still showing: *Les Belles de Noël*—Violet & Hope Fields. I've got a mental picture of it; and Jean-Louis has dozens of souvenir posters for us. "Farewell to the Métropole," I say as we drive away.

"The Métropole was good to us. We'll be back at Easter," Hope says.

26

Fouquet's at eleven o'clock at night throbs with chatter and laughter of media and show-biz people. The maître d'hotel greets us with the reverent bow I imagine he gives celebrities like Jessye Norman and Jeanne Moreau. He guides us through the main dining room where every table is occupied. Scanning the room for the rich and famous, I notice some guests are staring at us. Our group is gathered in an intimate gem of a dining room—wood paneled, warm, rosy lighting, sparkling with crystal glassware and silver ice buckets.

When I enter with Hope, Monique, and Odile, Jean-Louis says, "Finally, *les Belles* have arrived. Please take your seats. *À table.*" Four round tables with eight chairs each. As I take Hampton's arm, we go to the nearest table. When I'm seated, others take their places: Hampton on my left, Marie next to him, then Stuart, Faith, Billy, and Hope fill in. The chair on my right is for Jean-Louis, who is overseeing the arrangement from the center of the room.

When everyone is seated, Jean-Louis joins us. Looking around, I say to him, "Suzanne Dupont isn't here."

"She is hosting *in absentia.*"

"Gérard, is he here? I want to meet him."

"He had to leave after the show to handle a problem at the cyber café he manages."

A waiter pours champagne. I don't refuse. Standing, his flute of champagne held high, Jean-Louis toasts in French and English the cast, my family, and me: "My thanks to a superb company of dancers, singers, actors. To Violetta, queen of the stage, to her niece and stage daughter, Hope, and their wonderful family who made the journey to

Paris. To our future together in a grand Easter show!"

The music of glasses clinking brings Odile to her feet. She recalls the day she brought Hope and me together. Her toast is to our future as costars. After a flurry of toasts from the other tables, with some effort, I raise myself and my glass.

I choke up before saying a word. Regaining my composure: "I want to offer a toast to those who came before us, cleared the path, making it possible for us to get here. To the parents of the young performers. To my sister, Marie, Hope's real-life mother, for giving life to Hope. To my brother, Hampton, the first to put me onstage. To my faithful friend and manager, Jean-Louis, for finding the path and walking it with me. And most of all, to the memory of Josephine Baker. If she hadn't cleared the path and lit the way, I would never have had all these years in Paris and onstage." Raising glasses, the gathering joins me in exclaiming, "To Josephine!"

Waiters bring the first course and interest shifts to tantalizing plates of smoked salmon wrapped around a salmon mousse, crowned with black caviar; a creamy dill paste painted around the dish is garnished with sprigs of dill. The conversation at our table turns to food. Marie asks Hampton if caviar is frequently found on tables in Russia. He chuckles, "Potatoes and cabbage are served much more often."

Billy says, "Since I'll never get to Russia, I'd like to know what you have at a typical dinner." Hampton, across the table, says, "Borscht, a soup served with meat-filled turnovers called piroshkis. For the main course one would have meat—kebabs, for example, or fish. You ought to visit Russia. You've come overseas to France." Looking more relaxed, Hampton pauses before saying, "Refresh my memory—and my appetite. What do you have for dinner in Louisville?"

"Not what we had as kids," Marie says. "We eat much better now."

"Better believe it," says Billy. "We eat from high on the hog now."

Hope and Faith exchange glances of embarrassment. Hope says, "It's going to be a night of down-home reveries."

"I loved Louisville's Derby Pie, a rich chocolate laced with bourbon. Can you still get it?" Hampton asks.

Faith says, "Mom makes the best Derby Pie. That's what we should have brought over."

I smile, amused by the thought of bringing a Louisville dessert to Paris.

Satisfaction with the salmon is obvious; the waiters take away emptied plates. A sommelier pours a red wine for Jean-Louis to taste. He swirls it around, then lifts the glass to his nose, sniffing it before taking a sip. Billy and Stuart pay close attention the ritual. On tasting it, Jean-Louis's face brightens. "A fine Châteauneuf-du-Pape," he says. The sommelier pours a glass for me. Again I don't refuse. Waiters return with the next course: slices of duck breast in a cassis sauce, its color complemented by julienne carrots and white asparagus tied with a bow of chives.

"I've never seen such beautiful food," Faith says into the mouthwatering bouquet rising from her plate. Comments on the food and wine—flavorsome, tasty, scrumptious, different—circle around the table. A purr of contentment and a long silence follow compliments about the meal.

A trolley laden with dozens of cheeses is rolled into the room. Beyond the cheese trolley stands the dessert trolley. I looked at the desserts on entering and I knew I'd have to choose between the raspberry Napoleon and the vacherin. I'm sure Dr. Chang would excuse my dietary violations tonight, if only he knew.

Before we finish dessert, members of the cast at the other tables prepare to leave. They part with promises of keeping in touch, hopes of working together again. Each one comes to our table to say good-bye to Jean-Louis, Hope, and me.

"The party's over," Faith says.

"And the after-party is beginning," Hope remarks. "The family party, a time to tell family stories. Tell us what it was like when you were kids together."

"Oh, no, I don't want to go there," I tell her. Turning to Hampton, I say, "We need to start at the time I lost contact with you, when your letters from Korea stopped."

"Before I tell you what happened, I want to hear from Marie and you. What can I tell my children about you?" He speaks slowly with a baritone's resonance, a voice accustomed to giving orders.

Marie straightens her back, clasps her hands, and clears her throat, as if she's about to address the National Assembly. She turns to Hampton. His eyes shift in her direction. She says, "As you all know, I was left behind, at home alone with Mama. After high school, I went off to college at Kentucky State. Mama died in my freshman year. Violet flew over, made arrangements for the funeral, she managed everything. Violet gave the house over to me, had it rented to provide income for me, and told me to go back to KSU and get my college degree, which I did— with honors."

Leaning across Hampton to speak to me, Marie says, "You were my guardian angel. You gave me the house and good advice, and made it possible for me to have a decent life. At the time, I didn't appreciate it fully, didn't understand why you lived overseas if you cared about me." She lets out a long breath. At last she's got it off her chest. I sigh, too, knowing, at last, that my advice and the house have been appreciated.

Hope is looking steadily at me. Faith's focus is on Marie, who continues, "I'd earned a teacher's certificate, so I returned to Louisville to teach. I was appointed to the fifth-grade class at Newberg School. I moved back into our house. Remember Lloyd Grayson?" Hampton nods. Hope and Faith look solemn at the mention of their father's name. "He was a good carpenter and builder. I hired him to fix up the house. He started courting me and we got married. Violetta Mae, that is, Violet, flew over to attend the wedding. She gave us a sterling silver tray that I've cherished." Hope nods at this.

"To make a long story short," Marie says, "finally we were blessed with these two wonderful daughters, but Lloyd didn't live long enough to see them grow up." She doesn't mention her scene at his funeral; and I'm relieved. I wonder how she remembers it or whether she remembers it at all.

Sorrowfully she says, "I was a widow for ten years. The support of my Alpha Kappa Alpha sorority sisters and other good friends helped me keep my head above water—so to speak." Marie pauses, then adds, "When Bill's wife passed on, he and I grew closer. We were married five years ago and have been living happily ever after." She ends with the smile a teacher gives a grade-school class when she finishes a reading and closes the storybook. Billy, pleased with her recitation, beams across the table at Marie.

With a sidelong glance my way, Hampton says, "Now tell us about your life."

"It's your turn, going youngest to oldest. Anyway, I'd rather tell you tomorrow when you come for lunch at my place, where I can show you my pictures and photo albums. So let's hear from you, Hampton."

He strokes his goatee and frowns, looks from face to face, as if seeking someone who can relate to what he's experienced.

In a near whisper, Marie says, "Elmer Lucas came through Louisville several years ago. He told me about your time together in the Korean prison camp."

"So Lucas went back to the States. I wondered what happened to him."

"Why didn't you come back?" says Marie.

His words come haltingly. "I'd had enough of bigotry in the Army. What was waiting for me back there? Mama's bitterness at home and, in the streets, trouble, poverty, and prejudice. So I decided a few years in Soviet Russia would be better than what I had to face in Louisville. Soviet agents said we could study Russian, get vocational training and government housing. I did not go to the Soviet Union planning to stay. But I knew, because I declined repatriation, I would not return to the States."

He pauses, maybe waiting for our reaction, or maybe searching for words. We're all leaning toward him, straining to hear. The silence is broken at last by Marie. "What happened when you got into Russia?"

"We were taken to a reservation near Moscow. Six of us—four blacks, all of us from the South—and two whites—both Yankees. We were housed in a dormitory, had Russian language classes and political orientation there. After six months, we were separated. I never saw the others again. Because I know horses, I was assigned to work with the Army cavalry."

"What was that political orientation about?" asks Stuart.

"It was about class conflict, class struggle, white racial imperialism, and colonialism. They gave us pamphlets on Marxism in English. We had instruction and discussions in study groups. I had known nothing about communism when joined the Army. I did not realize we Negroes were colonized inside America. We were made to fight against people who stood for a collective system more beneficial to us than the American capitalist system. Understand?"

Stuart nods as if he understands. I wonder whether he does. Hampton's talk makes me wish I'd learned something about communism and the Cold War. I'd heard Josephine was called a communist for being against segregation in America, but she wasn't. She was an activist for civil rights. I'm thinking I should've been an activist or at least useful in the Civil Rights Movement. Going to a few Paris rallies wasn't much of a contribution.

Billy, agitated, is on the edge of his chair. "Damn, man, didn't you know you were being brainwashed?"

"I was brainwashed in Louisville and in the Army. You might say I was brain rinsed in Russia."

Billy, more agitated, is about to say something else. Obviously disturbed by the tone of their talk, Marie says, "Was it easy to adjust to life there?"

"At first, it was very hard—hard to learn Russian and hard to fit in. I tried to imitate their gestures,

219

ways of acting in public, tried to become Russian. It was pitiful. Laughable," he chuckles.

"How did that make you feel?" I ask, remembering how foolish I felt when I began speaking French and tried to act like the French.

"I felt inferior in a new way. Culturally inferior. They had their Old World traditions. Their old ways seemed better than American ways. Then I retreated into being myself." He smiles like he's thinking of some good times. "Some people took an interest in me because I'm black and American. They always asked about race relations in America. Some thought slavery was still going on, and I had to correct them. In a strange way, it made being American matter more to me."

I tell him, "I know exactly what you mean. Only when I came to Paris was I made to feel American. It's funny that you have to leave your country to find out what your country means to you, to feel it's actually a part of you."

Hampton nods and says, "I understood I would always be known as American, always be an outsider. My Russian is still limited. I still don't get everything I hear on radio or television or in some conversations. Anyhow, I am not included in some conversations. But my English got better. When I speak with people learning English, I must use good English."

"Your name—Tomas Mikhail Grischevich—did you change your name to make life easier?" I ask and then add, "Don't get me wrong. You know I changed mine, too."

"I started using the name as a joke. Not looking like somebody with that name amused some people. Or confused them. I realized an alias was a means of hiding from the authorities. And even hiding from myself." Brooding, he covers his mouth with both his hands as if he does not want to say more.

And so I say, "Well, now you're out of hiding. You've got no need to hide anything from us."

"It was more inventing than hiding. I invented a new self. I made up stories about my past, never telling the full story to my wife and children. The children know I have sisters, but with no pictures, no evidence of my family, they must have suspicions."

Stuart says, "I didn't bring my camera tonight, but tomorrow I'll take lots of pictures."

"We should have brought you pictures of Louisville," Marie says. "If you'd come back to Louisville, you'd find things quite different. You can make a good living there now, live in the suburbs, and the schools are better. Whites have become mannerly and respectful, even when waiting on us in restaurants, drugstores, banks, and so on."

Billy adds, "We enjoy the good life. Own a fine home, two cars—two Mercedes, in fact. Get good seats at the Derby and the Preakness, travel around the country, stay in first-class hotels. Man, your sister and I are living the American dream. You need to come back to Louisville and see how things have changed."

Hampton says, "You and Marie moved up into the black bourgeois class. But how many blacks in the States are still trapped in shacks and tenements, are unemployed or in jail, living the American nightmare? I have wondered what kind of situation I might have found for myself in Louisville."

Like Hampton, I, too, have imagined the turns and twists my life might have taken there. There was nobody in Louisville to help me into show business. That's why I'm troubled by Marie thinking Hope can make something of her talent there. Maybe I'll tell them just that tomorrow.

"You can't tell me you don't wish you were back home, Hampton. You must miss the action at the track, hanging out, just being with your own people," Marie insists.

"I used to wonder what was going on back home. I'd try to find something—anything—about Louisville in the news. I get news of Derby winners on the Internet. But being away so long, frankly, I have lost interest in Louisville."

"You must miss the excitement around Derby time," Billy says. "Does being a black American on the Russian horse scene make you feel exotic? I bet you're making history there."

"Jimmy Winkfield, the last black jockey to win the Kentucky Derby—won it in 1901 and '02—made racing history in Russia long before my time. He broke records in America and all across Europe. In Russia he staked out space for black Americans in racing."

"I guess he did for racing there what Josephine Baker and jazz musicians did for us in entertainment here," I say.

"Is racing important in Russia like it is in Louisville?" Billy asks.

"Moscow's Hippodrome is a major racetrack. Troika racing is much more popular there than flat-track racing. Huge crowds go to the Hippodrome, drink vodka between races, place bets with illegal bookies, and gamble in the casino. Racing is very popular."

While a waiter takes orders for cognac and cordials, Hope has a chance to say, "I'd like to know how you met your wife and hear about your children—my Russian cousins." Totally disarming, she makes Hampton smile.

"I wish your cousins could have seen your show tonight. They adore music and theater. You remind me of my daughter, Natasha."

"Is she the one with children?" I ask, trying to recall what he told me about his kids.

"No, Natasha was married, but has no children. My son, Anatoly, works in Siberia in forest management. He is not yet married, no children. It is Irina, the physician, who has two sons. I have pictures of the boys." From the breast pocket of his brown tweed jacket, he pulls out photos. "These are Irina's sons." He passes a picture to Marie. Handing another to me, he says, "And this was Svetlana." A plump blond probably in her late fifties at the time, holding a cigarette, glamorous in the style of Shelley Winters or Simone Signoret, she looks like she was robust and healthy.

"You said she died last year. Cancer?" I'm guessing.

"Yes. Breast cancer. Health care for women declined after the collapse of communism. It was difficult to get regular chemotherapy sessions. Even with Irina's medical connections, it was very difficult."

"You haven't told us how you met her," Hope says.

"Horses brought us together. You can count on finding happiness through horses." He smiles broadly, showing the Garfield gap between his front teeth. "Working at the cavalry's headquarters had its reward. I served under Igor Pinsky, a cavalry general and a Party member. Certain privileges came with his rank. When he retired, he had me assigned to the

223

government stable he managed. He and his wife, Anna, took an interest in me."

"So they introduced you to a Russian woman?" Marie interrupts.

"Not exactly. By taking an interest, I mean they admired my handling horses and respected my intelligence. The Pinskys took me to ballets and concerts, introduced me to Russian music. Anna Pinsky, Igor's wife, had studied English. She gave me books in English by Russian authors. She told me Alexander Pushkin was Afro-Russian, and gave me a book of his poems in English.

"The Pinskys had three sons and a daughter, Svetlana. They called me their fourth son, even before I met Svetlana. She was away in training for the Soviet Equestrian Olympic Team. When she returned, we met on horseback. Riding on the same trail, but in opposite directions, we met. I changed direction and followed her. She was an elegant rider, a woman of many talents, a good mother and wife. Her soul was wide and open, generous and sincere."

Faith's curiosity surfaces. "The family—her parents— did they approve of your marriage?"

"Yes, and they were proud of our children."

"Race wasn't a problem?" Billy asks.

"No, not for the Pinskys. But race matters in Russia. In general, Russians disapprove of interracial unions. Their ideal is for Russians to marry Russians, not marry foreigners regardless of race. My daughters, when you meet them, can tell you something about that."

"What would they say?" Faith asks.

"Natasha, because she is dark, has known rejection. Her marriage failed because her mother-in-law and her husband's sisters rejected her. They said their family would be disgraced if she had children, that is, children who were dark like her."

"What about your other daughter?" Hope wonders.

"Irina is fair-skinned with kinky hair. In school, girls made jokes about her hair. She still struggles with her appearance."

"Your son, how's he been treated?" Billy asks.

"Anatoly has his mother's looks: fair skin, blue eyes, blond hair. He's taken for Russian. He can pass."

"Cognac and cordials," our waiter announces. He makes the rounds pouring for the men, after all the women, including me, decline.

Glancing at his watch, Billy says, "I know it's getting late. But tell us how you've come to have a horse farm."

"When communism collapsed, many collectives also collapsed. The Pinskys acquired the stable when property was privatized. A year later, Igor Pinsky died. Svetlana's brothers, engineers with no interest in horses, yielded their shares in the enterprise to us. I took on a partner, a younger man, reliable, energetic. Next year, when Anatoly's contract with the forestry program ends, he will join us, work at the horse farm. I hope to acquire more land, expand the farm, and pass the business on to Anatoly."

Marie says, "You sound settled there and satisfied. But there must be moments when you wish you were back in America—maybe not in Louisville, but somewhere in the good ole USA."

"I have thought that if I got seriously ill, I would want to return so that in my native language I could be fully understood. But that will not happen. My children are Russian. They are bilingual; they understand me well enough. They will care for me.

As for being satisfied, I am not. I worry about prospects for the farm. An underworld element wants to control breeding and racing. It could become difficult for me and later for Anatoly. Still, I will remain in Russia. It is a matter of where I feel I am treated with dignity and respect, and appreciated for my skills, without being limited by my race."

I blurt out, "Amen, brother! That's how I feel in Paris."

"I cannot forget how we were treated in Louisville and what I experienced in the Army," he says, closing his eyes for a moment, grimacing as if in pain. "And over the years, I have heard about racial incidents, hate crimes, police brutalizing blacks, and fear of terrorism. Nothing that I hear or read about that country makes me want to return."

Hampton is telling them what I've felt in my heart for many years. He's my kindred spirit, my soul's true brother. Like me, he's come to terms with being an expatriate. He's a wise, seasoned man. He's learned a great deal from where he's lived. I want to know more about what life has taught him. I wonder why he's so cautious, what he fears about exposure. How can US authorities bring him down now? I'll ask him tomorrow. He's given us enough to sleep on tonight.

27

The racket of the neighbors throwing open shutters and rolling up steel grills on shop windows wakes me up. Another day on rue Frochot is underway.

I don't feel like getting up. The morning after a show closes always finds me in the doldrums. I know every show could be my last when the final curtain falls, the lights are switched off, and the posters are taken down. Every farewell cast party could be the end of all cast parties. But what a party, what a night! Being with Hampton and Marie brought back memories locked away in a trunk stored in the attic of my childhood. I may have to unpack them today. That could make for trouble because Marie and I don't remember things in quite the same way.

Marie has mellowed, become caring and gentle. I like her more now. Hampton understands himself and has come to terms with the way his life has played out. My life here has been justified. I want more time alone with Hampton before he has to leave.

After all the dancing I did, I'm riddled with aches and pains. Where did the impulse to dance across the stage in the finale come from? Kicked up these legs last night, and I can't lift them off the bed this morning. My cane. I think I left it at the party. I sure need it now. I can make it to the bathroom, though, holding on to things here and there.

"*Bonjour*, Josephine. Thanks for being with me last night. *Merci beaucoup.*" I blow a kiss to her altar as I pass into the living room where Hope is sleeping on the sofa bed. Looking down at her, my resident Sleeping Beauty, I don't see the little end table, bump into it, and almost lose my balance. "Oops," I gasp, waking up Hope. Without opening her eyes, she tells me it's too early to be up and about.

"Well, I'm getting an early start. I'm going to take a shower and do my makeup. I want to be ready for lunch today. Or did I dream they're in Paris and coming for lunch?"

"You didn't dream it. They're not coming until noon, hours from now. I need a little more sleep," Hope says, turning away and pulling the blanket over her head. As quietly as I can, I make my way to the bathroom, getting there not a second too soon. Timing the trip so that I get to the toilet before peeing on the floor has become my morning melodrama. Relieved, bladder empty, I sit a while—sort of meditating. The entire routine—toilet time, bathing, brushing teeth, fixing my hair, taking inventory of signs of aging, putting on my morning makeup, swallowing and injecting medicine—takes nearly an hour. I need a head start on the day.

***

In the kitchen, Leo waits to be fed. I fill his dish. Watching Leo eat makes me hungry. From the refrigerator, I take out a bowl of black olives and a chèvre log. We're out of coffee. I'll make a cup of tea. A cup of Earl Grey, olives, and cheese with yesterday's baguette, a good breakfast. I fill the kettle and turn on the gas. While the water heats, I make a list of things we need for lunch: six roasted chickens, three prepared salads, oak leaf lettuce, tomatoes, bread, coffee; and, from the patisserie, fruit tarts and chocolate mousse cake. Jean-Louis will bring champagne.

In the dining room, I notice Hope's already laid out a white tablecloth, dishes, platters, glasses, and napkins, all borrowed from André's café. She brought home the bouquets presented to us and put them in carafes. I move one of them, red and white roses with baby's breath, to the center of the dining table. It's going to be a beautiful *déjeuner*.

Tiptoeing into the living room, I stop to look at the array of pictures, hoping Hampton and Marie will take time to notice scenes from my life in the photographs. I wish now I'd put up some of Stanley's pictures alongside mine. Stanley never had the chance to meet anyone in my family; and I never met any of his folks. No acquaintance with in-laws or in-law problems. Maybe it was better that way. But I wish Stanley could have known Hampton. They probably would have been good buddies. And if Hope had come along when Stanley was alive, it might have eased his guilt and pain about distance from his daughter. There I go, slipping into my "if only" mode.

Hope looks snug, the blanket now tucked under her chin. She's sleeping in her earrings, the fake pearls that dangle. And she's smiling like she's enjoying a nice dream. If only she'd wake up. I want to talk with her about last night. If the hissing of the radiators and the wind rattling against the windows don't wake her up, I don't know what will.

Moving on into the bedroom, I decide I'll wear the sage Chanel suit. I take the suit from the armoire, lay it on the bed, and sit down beside it, admiring it. It's a lovely souvenir of my acquaintance with Suzanne Dupont. She and Henri Breton were very pleased with the production. Jean-Louis thinks they're ready to invest in an Easter show.

I better start getting dressed. It would be just like Marie to come early to catch me in my natural state. I don't want her to find me in this old, frayed kimono and worn-out slippers.

I get up, slip out of the kimono, and feel it fall around my feet on the floor. I'm suddenly dizzy and tired to the bone. My vision is blurred again. Still in my nightgown, I get back into bed. I'll feel better if I lie down for a few minutes.

I cover myself with the duvet, careful not to upset the Chanel suit. Right away, I'm falling asleep.

The next thing I hear is the phone ringing, and at the same time, somebody's knocking on the door. "Hope, wake up. Answer the door. I'll get the phone." I hear her feet hit the floor and scamper to the door. I pick up the receiver.

"*Bonjour.* Hello." No answer. I clear my throat, and again say, "*Bonjour.* Hello?"

I hear someone breathing. Music begins. Josephine sings "*J'ai deux amours, / Mon pays est Paris / Par eux toujours, / Mon coeur est ravi.*" Is it a recording? It can't be her voice. Or can it be? The music stops.

"*Allo. Qui est la?*" I call into the phone. No answer, no breathing, nothing. I hang up, thinking I must have imagined the call. I hear Hope talking to someone. Sitting up in bed, I call to her, "Hope, who was at the door?"

"Jean-Louis with Vladimir and two cases of champagne," she says.

"*Bonjour,* Violetta. How is our brightest star this morning?" Jean-Louis calls from the living room. Looking in and finding me in bed, he says, "You are still *déshabillée.* Are you going well?"

"I'm not myself."

"That does not surprise me. Your performance was stunning last night. You gave it all you had. I have brought the newspapers with the reviews. You will feel better when you read them. I asked Hope to buy *Paris Match,* several copies, when she goes to the *épicerie. Paris Match* has a feature article about you and the show with great pictures. Are you getting yourself up?" he asks from the foot of my bed.

"I've been up, but as I said, I'm not myself."

"*Alors*, I am not myself either. Vladimir is not gentle like my old Boris. He is wicked. I have not the patience and strength I used to have. I needed help to bring the champagne up the stairs."

"Did André help you?"

"No, it was Gérard. He drove me here and carried the cases up your stairs."

"Gérard is here? I want to meet him, thank him for finding Hampton."

"Gérard has already gone. I thanked him for you. I bought a present for him, the latest BlackBerry, and told him it was from you."

"I'll pay you for it now. And for the champagne, too."

"Not now. I will add it on your account."

Hope comes in, wrapped from her chin to her ankles in a new ruby sweater-knit coat. On her it looks chic. I'd look like an Alsatian sausage in it. She tells us she's going to do the errands.

To Jean-Louis she says, "Keep an eye on Vladimir. He's sniffing the cheese platter on the kitchen table."

"Do not forget the *Paris Match*," Jean-Louis reminds her as she's leaving. "*Alors*, I must watch Vladimir. Violetta, you must get dressed." He closes the door, allowing me more time to sleep.

***

I'm awakened by noises from the kitchen—Vladimir's bark, Leo's screech, excited sounds in Hope's voice, Jean-Louis crowing. I open my eyes, look about, and listen.

"The pictures in *Paris Match* are fabulous!" Hope says, skipping into the bedroom. Right behind her Jean-Louis, arms laden with newspapers, says, "You must read these reviews. The critics want another show—my Easter show."

They sit on my bed, Hope on one side and Jean-Louis on the other. Hope shows me the article in *Paris Match*. Jean-Louis spreads open the papers, turning pages to the reviews. He translates headlines, captions on photos, and excerpts in bold print: "Sensational Fields Family Show; Violet Fields Never Better; Violet and Hope Fields, New Mother-Daughter Team Triumph; Holiday Show Draws Standing Ovations; A Song and Dance Partnership for All Seasons—Violet and Hope; Violet Fields' Amazing Return; America's New Black Hope; Orchids for Violet; Marvelous Music, Heavenly Fields." Jean-Louis and Hope take turns reading aloud. I'm luxuriating in the feeling it gives me, hearing the critics' praise. They pass pages to me. I put on my glasses and read what I've heard.

The clock of Saint Pierre rings out its musical chimes. I count its striking twelve. "It is noon," Jean-Louis notices. "Your family will arrive soon. I will help Hope. You must now get up and dressed."

"I don't feel like leaving this bed covered with beautiful reviews. I want to read them again. And I want Hampton and Marie and Faith to see them."

"I bought enough papers for the whole party," says Hope. "I will translate the best reviews for them."

A knock at the door and Vladimir barks. "Already someone is here," Jean-Louis says. "I will hold the hound. You go to the door, Hope." He leaves and closes the bedroom door, leaving me alone with the newspapers.

I know three or four folks have arrived. I hear them, but not well enough to make out who is here. When they come into the living room, I can hear them: Marie talking with Hope or Faith. Their voices are similar. Men laughing. Billy Knox and Stuart amused by something.

"Someone is at the door," Marie says.

"I'll get the door," Hope says. Voices in the living room are hushed. Moments later Hope is greeting people and inviting them to meet the others. I hear Hope introduce André and his mother to Marie and Bill, Faith and Stuart. So everyone, except Hampton, has arrived. Jean-Louis, sounding very jolly, offers champagne.

Marie asks when I'll be joining the party. Jean-Louis, almost shouting so I will hear him, says, "She is getting dressed. She will make an entrance soon."

I turn over and try lifting the duvet and newspapers off me, but I just can't muster the effort. I think of Josephine in her final hours surrounded by newspapers with rave reviews of her Bobino show.

I'll rest until Hampton comes. Then I'll get up. The chatter of small talk continues in the next room. During a lull in their conversation, there's a knock, loud as a stage knock, at the door. "That must be Hampton," Hope says. Her high-heeled footsteps are in the hall. A man's voice. Yes, it is Hampton.

Like a chorus greeting the hero in an opera, I hear his name in several voices: "Hampton. Hampton, Hampton, Hampton!" He speaks quietly, cordially to all. A pause, and he asks, "Where is Violetta Mae?"

"She is preparing to make her entrance," Jean-Louis says. "While we are waiting, have some champagne." He uncorks a bottle. A lovely sound. Over the clink of glasses, Marie says, "To Hope's future onstage in Paris."

Hampton adds, "And a toast to Violet—our own Violetta Mae, leading lady and superstar, brightest in the firmament."

Hope taps gently on the bedroom door and says, "Five minutes, Miss Fields."

"I'm getting ready. I'm coming." I sit up but fall back onto the pillow, feeling drowsy.

Moments later Hope comes into my bedroom, saying, "I'm here to help you."

Above the altar is a blinding burst of light. From the center of the light steps Josephine draped in a long, white robe. In an instant, she's sitting on my bed humming "Steal Away." Her perfume is in the air. Standing at my bedside, Hope is utterly still. Josephine sings softly, "Steal away, / steal away/ steal away to Jesus / Steal away / steal away home/ I ain't got long to stay here. / My Lord calls me / He calls me by the thunder / The trumpet sounds it in my soul/ I ain't got long to stay here." When her singing ends, I hear a solo trumpet playing in Stanley's style a swinging "Steal Away."

I feel Hope's hand holding mine. Josephine has me by the other hand. Josephine draws me away. I see Hope's smile. I blink. I see Hope's tears. It's getting dark. The music ends. I close my eyes. The curtain falls.

A NOTE ABOUT THE AUTHOR

Florence Ladd's novel, *Sarah's Psalm* (Scribner), received the 1997 best fiction award from the American Library Association's Black Caucus. Her poems have been published in *The Women's Review of Books, The Progressive, The Rockhurst Review, Sweet Auburn, Beyond Slavery* and *Transition.* With Marion Kilson, she is the co-author of *Is That Your Child? Mothers Talk about Rearing Biracial Children.* She lives in Cambridge, Massachusetts and Flavigny-sur-Ozerain, France.

This book's typeface:

Bookman Old Style, a serif typeface designed by Alexander Phemister in 1858 for the Miller andRichard foundry. Several American foundries copied the design, including the American Type Founders, who changed the name to Bookman Oldstyle, as an alternative to Caslon, with straighter serifs, making it more suitable for book applications.

This book was designed by Halstead Harris.